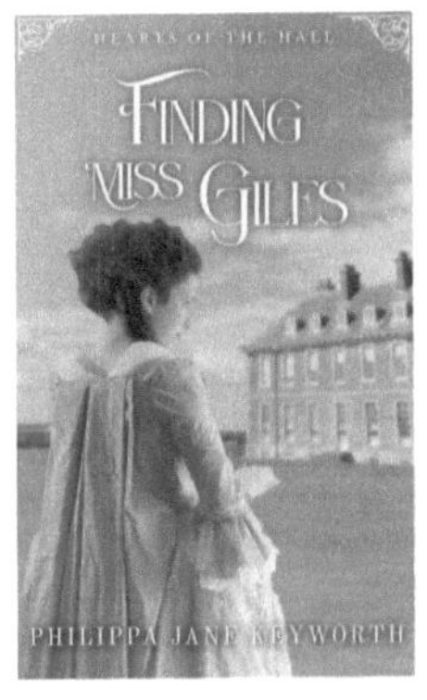

ONE HOUSE.
THREE GENERATIONS.
SIX UNFORGETTABLE CHARACTERS.

Spanning the Georgian, Regency and Victorian generations of the Derringer family, the *Hearts of the Hall* series follows the women who capture the hearts of the Derringer gentlemen.

Get swept away in the romance, misunderstandings, secrets and happily-ever-afters of this faith-based, multi-author series by Philippa Jane Keyworth, Rachel Knowles, and Edwina Kiernan.

FINDING MISS GILES	*Philippa Jane Keyworth*	1780
ENGAGING MISS SHAW	*Rachel Knowles*	1815
RESTORING MISS HASTINGS	*Edwina Kiernan*	1850

HEARTSOFTHEHALL.COM

FINDING MISS GILES

PHILIPPA JANE KEYWORTH

PASSALANDE
BOOKS

ISBN (eBook): 978-1-7397076-2-0

ISBN (Print): 978-1-7397076-3-7

Cover design by: Philippa Jane Keyworth

Editing by: Rachel Knowles

Formatting by: Edwina Kiernan

CONTENTS

*For the Lord, who is my home, and whose steadfast
love has kept my feet on solid ground during all
the storms of life.*

FINDING MISS GILES

CHAPTER 1

*M*iss Araminta Giles was nobody's fool. She prided herself—at one-and-twenty— on having an exceptionally sharp wit. It had been honed throughout her formative years and she thanked God for it. There was no one else in the world to care for her. It was that wit which had first alerted her to the prying nature of her travelling companion today.

"Have you no chaperone with you?" asked the woman sitting opposite her in the stagecoach.

Ary did not miss her accusatory tone, nor the way the middle-aged woman raised her nose a little and sniffed.

"No," Ary replied, wishing for the umpteenth time that she had taken a seat on the roof of the carriage rather than inside.

Outside the carriage was not a desirable location, and a kind man travelling from Sussex had offered her his seat inside when she had joined the stage in Ludgershall. She had taken up the offer, happy not to be subjected to the elements, not knowing she would be subjected to the interrogation of one Mrs Dibley instead.

"Well, well, well." The woman sucked in air between her teeth. "My husband, who is the vicar of St Mary's Charlcombe, would never have *me* travelling alone. No, my dear, not I." Mrs Dibley shook her head in a patronising manner. "That is why you came with me, isn't it, Lily?" she said, turning her beady eyes on the timid, young girl sitting next to her.

The housemaid nodded but was precluded from speaking by her mistress' next question to Ary.

"And where is it that you are travelling alone, young lady?"

The memory of Ary's school teacher came vividly to her mind. Miss Drench had used a similar tone when addressing her pupils.

The thought of her old school mistress set Ary's mind on a different course from answering Mrs Dibley's prying questions. If Miss Drench could see her now, travelling to be a lady's companion to a gentleman's daughter near Bath, she would be thrilled. Though she would not have shown it. Miss Drench had never revealed her emotions to her charges. She was as stern a woman as Ary had ever met, but she had also been frank with her opinions, and had assured Ary that she was made for more than scrubbing floors and banking fires.

"Near Bath," Ary replied, unwilling to give in to this woman's questioning and also rather curious as to what her reaction would be when Ary gave her less than helpful answers.

She was rewarded with another sucking in of breath

between Mrs Dibley's teeth and a look akin to that which someone would wear when smelling something foul. Ary kept her countenance impassive and turned back to the window.

There were times she missed her old school teacher. When Ary had shown promise she was plucked from the ranks of the Foundling Hospital's orphans at the age of nine—thanks to a financial benefactor—and placed in a charity school. Miss Drench had delivered all Ary's schooling there before installing her young charge as a teacher herself in the same school.

Ary had left all that behind when she had been appointed a companion to Mrs Stanaway of Edge House. Being that Ary had neither enquired after the position, nor knew the lady to whom she was to be engaged, she had been sceptical of the offer of employment.

But Miss Drench had said, in her pragmatic way, that Miss Giles should be grateful for the opportunity and show less of a mind to question it. Ary had agreed with Miss Drench. It was too good an offer to pass up, so she had accepted the position.

After little more than eighteen months, Mrs Stanaway had taken ill and expired. Ary had been sorry for it. The woman had been sharp and demanding, but a fair employer, and had exposed Ary to the social mores and niceties of polite Society. Not only that, Ary had even received a wage. It was meagre, but more than the bed and board she had received at the charity school. Ary had been trying to save it, though it barely stretched further than weekly items she came in need of.

The loss of her employer was also the loss of her home and security, and Ary had been fearing she would have to return to the charity school when an unexpected letter had arrived. A respectable family was looking for a companion for the young lady of the house, to accompany her in Bath Society before she made her debut in London. A mutual acquaintance of Mrs Stanaway had recommended Ary to them. Another providential happenstance, and Ary had again taken Miss Drench's words to heart and accepted the engagement. It might only be for a short period—they may not even like her—but it would do for now.

So here she was, travelling alone to her new employment. After all, an orphan left at the Foundling Hospital as a babe was still an orphan at one-and-twenty, and had no means to travel with company even if she should wish it.

"Ah, not further on to Gloucestershire then," Mrs Dibley said, breaking in on Ary's thoughts after only a few moments. "My husband and I are very familiar with the Bath area. Where is it you're travelling to? I'm sure we will know of it."

As if that would make any difference, thought Ary. After this journey she would likely never see Mrs Dibley again. With that in mind, and seeing the keen look on Mrs Dibley's face, Ary finally relented.

"Duriel Hall," she said.

"Duriel Hall." Mrs Dibley gasped the words. "*Duriel Hall,*" she said again, this time with a tone of reverence.

Ary withdrew her gaze from the window and looked with marginally more interest at Mrs Dibley's unfolding reaction. Her destination was well known then.

Mrs Dibley rocked on her seat, Ary presumed with glee. "What a place to be going. My husband was great friends with the old Mr Derringer," she said. Her chin came up proudly. "And he has known the young Mr Derringer and his sister since they were babes in arms."

Ary recognised the name. The young Mr Derringer in question was the gentleman who had written to offer her employment—as companion to his sister. To be engaged as a companion once was unusual for a foundling, and now twice? Mr Derringer knew nothing of her. The question which had gnawed at her, and she had been persistently batting away, came back to mind. Why had he chosen her as a companion for his sister?

The uneasy feeling led Ary to one conclusion: she should not trust that this engagement would offer any more security than the last. All good things—Ary had learned in her short time on this earth—came to an end. And that was if any good thing came at all.

"You are to be a scullery maid, perhaps?" Mrs Dibley asked, looking disapprovingly at Ary's patched cloak, and the faded fabric of her day dress peeking from beneath it.

Mrs Stanaway had only allowed Ary two plain dresses to be made up at the old woman's expense. One for daily wear and another for Sundays or when they went into company. Ary's employer saw no sense in spending money on anything but what she considered essential, and Ary's small wage had not been sufficient to pay for any more items of clothing. After a year and a half of solid use, the only dresses Ary owned were showing their age.

"They need many such maids to run an establishment like the Hall," said Mrs Dibley when the object of her interrogation did not immediately answer.

Ary had wondered, when she had read the name Duriel Hall, whether a hall was very much bigger than a house. Mrs Stanaway's home, Edge House, had seemed a grand place when Ary had first arrived. From Mrs Dibley's response to her destination, Ary imagined the Hall would have an equal effect on her. Perhaps she might turn the tables and gain information of her own from this woman.

"I am engaged for employment," she said evasively, allowing a lilt into her voice to disguise the elocution Miss Drench had been so insistent on during her schooling. "Is it a very big place? Only I 'ave had trouble before, finding my way around some 'ouses."

Ary smiled inwardly. She had always enjoyed participating in small performances they had put on at the Foundling Hospital to occupy the children.

"*Very* large, my child," said Mrs Dibley, a tone of condescension back in her voice.

Good, thought Ary. That tone showed that Ary's little ruse had been accepted. Mrs Dibley now 'understood' where Ary sat on the social strata, and it was decidedly lower than herself.

Underestimation, Ary had learned from a young age, was a unique weapon when facing the world.

"It dates right back to the 1400s, before Henry VII, though the house that is there now was built in the 1720s by Mr Derringer's grandfather. It is a fine building, a fine one. My husband has been there above three times, you know." She took on the appearance of a cat who had just brought in a dead mouse to its owner. "It has been home to the Derringers throughout that time. Though you will likely not see much of them below stairs." Mrs Dibley sniffed again, and Ary realised it was the action she took when setting someone else down.

"Would you be able to tell me then, what the master is like, as I'm not like to see him when I am there. Be they good people?" The phrasing of that last question made Ary cringe, but the play-acting was entirely convincing the vicar's wife.

The woman smiled patronisingly at Ary. "The best of the quality, or so my husband says. Mr Derringer is a God-fearing man and a kind master. You should consider yourself excessively fortunate to be engaged in such a place."

"Oh, I do, Mrs Dibley, I do." Ary nodded vigorously, so that it looked as if her head might fall right off her shoulders. "Thankee for making me aware of how thankful I should be."

There was the glimmer of suspicion in Mrs Dibley's eyes. Was her game up? Ary turned back to the window before Mrs Dibley could stare at her any longer. It was just as well for her stomach was lurching again. She didn't travel well.

Through the grimy panes of glass she saw buildings passing by. At some point during the interrogation from the inquisitive Mrs Dibley, they had arrived on the outskirts of Bath. A short time later they reached the staging post, and the creaking carriage came to a halt.

There was a great deal of shouting outside the vehicle as ostlers came out. The clipping of wooden soled boots on worn flagstones. The hollow thuds and scrapes of trunks being removed from the roof of the vehicle.

In the midst of this cacophony, one of the ostlers appeared on the other side of Ary's window. They opened the door, a gust of fresh air a welcome relief, and handed down Mrs Dibley, her housemaid and finally Ary.

"It will be a long walk to Duriel Hall for you, child,"

Mrs Dibley said, turning to Ary after snapping at the groom to handle her luggage with more care.

In all fairness, he had just dropped it worryingly close to a pile of horse manure.

"Thankee, Mrs Dibley, I shall find my way."

"It will no doubt keep you healthy, all that exercise. My husband will be picking me up in our little carriage."

As if on cue, a pony and cart came around the side of the inn, driven by an excessively round-faced gentleman.

"Geraldine!" called the gentleman, not paying attention to where his pony was going and allowing it to dive straight towards a pile of hay thrown out for the stage horses.

One of the inn's grooms shouted from an open stable, running out to shoo the animal away from the food. There was a general commotion while the cart was moved away, which the gentleman driver seemed unperturbed by, smiling all the while. Once the cart was settled on the far side of the yard, Mrs Dibley's husband climbed down in an ungainly fashion and came towards his wife with open arms.

"Husband!" said Mrs Dibley, stretching out her hands.

For a brief moment Ary forgot the woman's irritating qualities and the corner of her mouth pulled up into a reluctant smile. How pleasant it must feel to arrive home and be welcomed by family.

She watched over the next half an hour as Mrs Dibley's luggage was unloaded from the stagecoach and placed carefully in the back of the generously described 'carriage'. It was little more than a flatbed cart with a driving seat. Ary wondered how the vehicle would be able to accommodate the trunk as well as its generously proportioned owners and servant. She soon saw the maid climbing up to perch precariously on the trunk and felt sorry for the poor girl.

"...a maid to the Derringers..."

The snippet drifted across the yard to Ary. She purposely gazed at a water trough and directed her ear to the ecclesiastical couple, attempting to hear the rest of the conversation.

"We will pass there on our way home. Why don't we take her up, my dear?"

"Oh no, Matthew, that would hardly do. Delivering a scullery maid to her new employment? It would not look at all well."

"But it's near on five miles to Duriel Hall, Geraldine."

"Matthew, I know you have no sensitivities to these niceties, but it really will not do. We cannot deliver scullery maids and expect to be invited to the Hall for a visit. No, my dear. She will do very well stretching her legs after such a journey."

The charitable thoughts Ary had allowed to dampen her dislike of Mrs Dibley evaporated. She looked directly across the yard and caught the eye of the vicar's wife, giving her the unrelenting hard stare she usually reserved for disobedient pupils.

Ary gave a smug smile when the overly confident woman looked away. She would have continued to stare had someone not called her name.

"Miss Giles!"

Ary turned to see a man dressed in livery walking around into the stable yard. She moved forward as the man called her name again.

"Are you Miss Giles, for Duriel Hall?"

"Yes."

"Mr Derringer has sent the carriage for you. I beg your pardon for not being here when the stage arrived. I had a time of it trying to find space for the carriage and had to pay a lad to hold the horses' heads on the road outside. There's a fair amount of traffic hereabouts."

Ary felt an immediate liking for this friendly man and pointed out her portmanteau when he asked her for her luggage.

"That all, Miss?" he asked, surprised not to be directed to a trunk as well.

"Yes, that's all."

"Very well." He bent down and picked up the portmanteau and then led the way out of the yard and around to the front of the building.

Ary could not resist directing a condescending smile towards Mrs Dibley as she passed her.

"Thank you for your conversation, Mrs Dibley," she said with perfect pronunciation.

The woman looked startled and was staring between Miss Giles and the coachman leading her out of the yard. Ary turned away and hoped she would not come across Mrs Dibley again.

***

"It'll be about half an hour's journey, miss." The coachman paused outside the door to the taproom. "Will you be wanting to rest at all before we set off? Mr Derringer instructed me to order you whatever refreshment you might require before going to the Hall."

Ary's fine dark brows rose. She would not have expected such solicitousness from her employer.

"I think I should like to carry on, if we may?"

"Of course, miss."

The driver handed her up into a mercifully empty carriage. Ary noted the fine upholstery and appreciated the cleanliness of the interior in comparison to the stage. They set off, the Derringer's carriage retracing the stagecoach's route until they were back in the Somerset hills.

Shortly after, the vehicle turned off the post road. The smaller byway made for a distinctly less comfortable journey. Ary had not travelled a great deal and her inability to absorb the bends and rises showed her greenness. Quite literally, in fact. For she was sure her complexion was far greener than normal. Another steep downhill came, and she gripped at the window frame to steady herself. At least on the declines the speed was substantially slower.

When the carriage was level again she ventured a look outside the window. The only view she was afforded was that of trees and the muddy banks of the road rising up beside the vehicle. They turned eastwards, the carriage hitting a rut in the road and sending Ary crashing against the side wall of the interior. She felt her stomach lurch and clapped her hand over her mouth. She breathed—in and out, in and out—willing the nausea to subside.

"Here it is, miss. Beyond the rise," the driver called from outside.

Ary shuffled closer to the window again. She released the lock and it dropped down with a clatter. A blast of fresh air hit her, cooling her face. When she opened her eyes again she caught sight of a house sat atop the rise the carriage was journeying around. A flutter of misgiving ran through her. She realised Mrs Dibley's over-enthusiastic words had not done the place justice.

The house rose three stories from its square footings, the neat red bricks and stone frieze above looking proudly out over the manicured lawns. As they drew nearer Ary could see more sash windows than she could count and a stone terrace stretching out on the west side. She thought she saw someone standing on it, but as they passed into the avenue of oak trees that led to the Hall's entrance, the trunks obscured whoever it was.

Ary looked down at her patched cloak and faded skirts and felt a clammy sweat breaking out on her palms. Duriel Hall was far grander than Edge House.

The sound of beaten track beneath the carriage wheels changed to gravel crunching. The sick feeling came back into her stomach, but this time it was not from the motion. She scolded herself inwardly, balling her hands into fists and looking again from the carriage window. She had borne far worse than a little luxury. She would not allow such a place and such people to overawe her. After all, they had chosen her, had they not? They knew she was a nobody from nowhere. Surely that was what they were expecting?

The carriage drew alongside a classically designed portico that stood on the north side of the Hall. A man and a woman stood outside, waiting to greet her. Before she could stop herself from the childish instinct, she jerked back against the carriage seat so that she would not be seen.

Unballing her hands, she reached for the little wooden heart she always wore around her wrist and pressed it between her finger and thumb. The familiar action soothed her and then, when the carriage drew to a halt, she took a deep breath.

The door opened and the steps were let down. She released the heart at the same time as her breath, and took the driver's hand to descend from the carriage and face her new home. All the while she reminded herself that a lack of fortune was not shameful. A lack of character was.

CHAPTER 2

William Derringer watched as the young, dark-haired woman was handed down from the carriage. The clouds, which had briefly hidden the sun's direct beams from the welcome party, moved off and bright light shone down just as Miss Giles stepped on the gravel and lifted her eyes to meet her employer.

The light dazzled her briefly and, as she adjusted to the brightness, William was afforded a moment to take her in. She was small, her figure fine, and dressed in a cloak that had seen better days. But her drab clothing did nothing to take away from her beauty. For that is what she was—beautiful. And William found himself startled by it.

He had expected her to be more akin to his sister Charlotte, plump in face, and with that childlike look which had not yet been shed. But Miss Giles, who was in all fairness several years Charlotte's senior, was nothing like a child. Her oval face was fair and clear, with fine brows arching above very dark eyes. He noted a full mouth and if he had not just appointed her as his sister's companion, he might have fancied himself moonstruck.

She was staring at him now, those dark eyes observing him with a look of wariness. He shook himself inwardly and stepped forward.

"Miss Giles."

He bowed low before her, hoping the action would allow him time to regain his equanimity. This was the last reaction he had expected to have on meeting Miss Giles.

"I am Mr Derringer," he continued. "This is my sister, Miss Derringer." He held out a hand to bring Charlotte out from under the portico, and onto the drive to greet her new companion.

"A pleasure, Miss G-Giles."

Charlotte always stammered when she was nervous. It was a habit William had hoped she would grow out of before her first season, but alas it had remained. Once Charlotte got to know someone, the stammer would slowly fade. She never exhibited one when speaking with William, unless she was very cross with him. But on coming out she would consistently be meeting with individuals with whom she was not acquainted, and William feared for what the stammer would do to her chances of finding a suitable husband.

That was what had prompted him to introduce his sister into Bath society first. It was quiet here at the moment, and she might make her debut slowly—and with more friends around her—than if she went straight to London. The appointment of Miss Giles, after the passing of their mother last year, was to facilitate this.

"Good afternoon," said Miss Giles, curtseying to them both very nicely.

At least, William thought with relief, Miss Giles had been schooled well despite her upbringing. It had been a gamble to engage her, but essential. He only hoped the gamble would pay off and his promise would be fulfilled.

"I h-hope your j-journey was not t-too taxing?" Charlotte asked.

"Thank you," said Miss Giles. "I have not travelled so far before, but it was quite agreeable."

She seemed unfazed by Charlotte's stammering and William was thankful for it. The affliction always grew worse when attention was drawn to it. Charlotte asked Miss Giles how long the journey had been, and William found himself staring unashamedly at the woman, observing how her long dark lashes brushed her cheeks as she blinked.

"William?" Charlotte said.

Both women were looking at him and he found himself caught out.

"I th-think perhaps Miss G-Giles would l-like to rest after her j-journey."

"Of course." William inclined his head, feeling a fool for staring so moon-faced at the woman and forgetting his duties as master of the house. "Jeffers, please bring the rest of Miss Giles' luggage into the house."

"This is it, sir," Jeffers said lamely, holding up an old portmanteau.

"You have no trunk?" William asked in surprise, looking back to Miss Giles.

He saw something flash in the woman's eyes and then her chin rose a little.

"No, I do not."

William lowered his brows and attempted to hide his response. He had inadvertently caused offence. But had she really no trunk? Did all the belongings this woman had in the world fit into so small a bag?

"Very well. Please, Miss Giles, if you will come with us."

He offered her his arm to go into the house, but she did not move. She looked between herself and the footman who waited beside the portico's pillars. There was an uncertain look in her expression. Had she expected to enter the house behind its master and mistress and not alongside them as a companion should?

"May I escort you?" He opened his arm wider.

Now her eyes moved between his arm and his face, her fine brows rising. Finally she nodded and stepped forward to take it. Her fingers rested so lightly it was as if they weren't there. Perhaps she was scared to touch him. After all, what men had this woman known in her life and how had she been treated before coming here? He could only guess.

"Welcome to Duriel Hall," he said.

Charlotte had fallen in step beside them, but was clearly too nervous to take Miss Giles' other arm.

"I hope you will enjoy your new home."

"Thank you," Miss Giles said in a voice barely above a whisper.

William glanced down at her and saw she was looking around herself. He slowed his step so that she could absorb her surroundings. As she did so, he saw her dark eyes widen, taking in the marble floor and stuccoed ceiling.

The brief entrance gave way to a great open space known as the inner hall in the centre of the house. William felt Miss Giles' hand disappear from his arm. She wandered forward, in an almost dreamlike state, looking up. Her eyes ran over the great paintings his grandfather had commissioned from an Italian artist who had been in London for many years and who had spent a year in residence at Duriel Hall during that time. Then her gaze fell to the black marble of the stair's balustrade, following it around the edge of the room and up to the first and second floors. He saw her eyes trace the gold leaf accenting the carvings on the marble. William had forgotten, having walked through this hall so many times since his youth, the impact it had been designed to have. He knew she had never seen the like before, and so saw it as the masterpiece it was.

A clock on a side table struck the half-hour and Miss Giles visibly jumped. Her head snapped round, and she caught him staring at her again. That was the third time. Three times too many, William scolded himself.

"Y-you'll have to f-forgive us, Miss G-Giles. It's our h-home so we have s-seen it so many t-times and don't notice its beauty," Charlotte said kindly.

"It is beautiful," Miss Giles concurred, her voice holding a note of reverence.

"Thank you," said William. "Our grandfather designed it. He rather liked to make an impact."

Charlotte chuckled, but Miss Giles looked uncertain.

"Here is the H-Hall's motto." Charlotte pointed up at carved words above one of the doorways.

William's eyes ran over the familiar lettering,

GOD IS MY HOME

"The meaning of Duriel," he offered, watching the changing looks of admiration on Miss Giles' face.

"I had wondered," Miss Giles said, her voice soft yet clear. "I have not come across the word before."

"Grandfather was a sc-scholar," Charlotte said. "He collected m-many of the b-books in the library."

"Library?" Miss Giles' eyes grew impossibly wider, and she looked at William for confirmation.

This time there wasn't just admiration in them, but eagerness. She was a reader then. Miss Drench had not been spinning false compliments in her letters.

"Yes," William confirmed. "Now, shall we have some refreshments?" He gestured to one of the many doors off the inner hall, and allowed Charlotte to lead the way into the rose drawing room, which overlooked the lawns on the south side of the Hall.

It was one of William's most-loved rooms. This was where he sat with Charlotte in the evenings. Where they could be comfortable together. While there were fine papers on the walls and a few ornaments, including a Boulle clock on the mantelpiece, the chairs in here were well worn and inviting, the rug before the fire thick and warm, and they could always be sure to find Jupiter, the ancient sighthound, sprawled on the hearth. He was there now, though he did not rise to greet his master, instead offering a slow thump of his tail.

William saw Miss Giles' eyes focus on the collection of books scattered on various side tables, tipping her head to read the spines in a manner she, no doubt, thought discreet. It was—but William was observing her more keenly than most. He had been waiting to meet Miss Giles for the past year.

Jupiter at last rose and padded over to greet the newcomer. Miss Giles stumbled back when he pushed his wet nose into her hand without invitation. Then she side-stepped straight into Mr Derringer. He was all too aware of her small figure pressing against him and instinctively reached up to take her arms and steady her, and himself.

"Pay no heed to Jupiter—he won't hurt you." William, stepping back, dropped his hands from Miss Giles and tried to drop the inappropriate thoughts from his head at the same time.

What was wrong with him? He was behaving as green as his sister might over a pair of fine eyes.

The woman was clearly unaware of the effect her proximity had on him for Miss Giles made no immediate move to put distance between them. Her head turned as she kept her eyes warily on the dog who was now padding around the chair to his master in the hopes of a more friendly reception.

When Jupiter reached William, and nuzzled his hand for an ear scratch, Miss Giles finally moved away to where his sister was sitting. It was only then that William realised he had been holding his breath. Dash it all! He had seen pretty women before. He rolled his shoulders back, trying to look like the master of the house as he attempted to control his feelings. There were things he should not forget where Miss Giles was concerned. He must remain objective in his assessment of her.

"There, there, boy," William murmured, his eyes still on Miss Giles as he addressed the dog. He gave him a final ear scratch and then commanded him to go and lay down.

The dog tried his chances, nosing him for another pet, but gaining no response he turned and went back to his warm patch of rug before the fire.

"We named him J-Jupiter in honour of our father

who had a f-fascination with ancient R-Rome after going on the Grand T-Tour," Charlotte explained to Miss Giles.

The woman's dark eyes were still watching the dog hesitantly.

"Call for refreshments will you, Charlotte?" William asked. "I'm sure Miss Giles will be desirous of a cup of tea before she is shown to her rooms to rest."

And perhaps, while she rested, William might be able to gain control over himself.

"Of course." Charlotte jumped up to ring the bell.

"Thank you," said Miss Giles, and then she began to ask Charlotte questions about her education and what she was looking forward to most about her first Season.

Charlotte, who was nervous at first and stammered a great deal, began to relax when Miss Giles made no comment on the stuttering. Soon she was chattering away, only now and then stumbling on her words.

When the tea arrived, Charlotte poured it as their mother had taught her to, and William felt a swell of pride. Her hand was steady and she did not spill a drop.

William joined in the conversation when required, but mostly stayed out of it, observing Miss Giles. Every so often, their eyes met, though—he noted—she chose not to keep his gaze for long.

When the tea was all drunk, and the bread and butter that had been served with it thoroughly demolished, the housemaid came to clear it away and William asked her to fetch Mrs Higgs.

"Will you show Miss Giles to her room, Mrs Higgs?" asked William when the housekeeper appeared.

"Yes, sir, of course, sir," the middle-aged woman's white cap bobbed furiously.

She began ushering Miss Giles from the room.

"We have unpacked your things, miss," William heard Mrs Higgs saying as both women passed before him. "And we can draw you a bath if you should be wanting one after your journey."

William missed Ary's murmured answer and soon both women had left the room, shutting the door behind them.

Charlotte turned beaming green eyes upon him.

"Oh, I like her, William."

He smiled, happy to see that his appointment of Miss Giles—despite his ulterior motives—had not displeased Charlotte.

"Good, I'm glad."

"Do you suppose she will like it here?"

"I am sure any companion of yours could be nothing but happy, Charlotte."

She wiggled her eyebrows at him in an unbecoming fashion.

"And you will not be too serious with her? You were staring at her so hard earlier that I thought she had done something you had taken exception too. I half thought you were going to scold her at any minute."

William felt the tips of his ears go warm.

"You don't disapprove of her do you?" Charlotte asked.

"No."

William's thoughts had been nothing but approving of Miss Giles—of her appearance at least—but that was hardly appropriate or to the point. It was her character he was interested in—and *that* had yet to be proven.

"Then you must stop looking as though you d-do,"

said Charlotte, a stammer slipping out as she scolded him.

William thought about his promise. It had all sounded so straightforward before he had met Miss Giles. But now? He had not expected her to be so... Would he be able to remain indifferent? The prospect seemed challenging, yet, if he did not manage it, his whole plan might fail.

CHAPTER 3

$\mathcal{M}$rs Higgs left Ary in her new room. Ary
stared at the room, which was twice the
size of any place she had slept before. She caught sight of
her portmanteau to the side of the dressing table and
came over to it, flipping back the lid and seeing an empty
interior. They had unpacked her things? She turned back
to the room, her chest feeling tight, her whole life had
been packed into that case.

As she turned, she glimpsed her nightgown and cap
laid out on the bed. She walked over to them, brushing
her fingers against the worn material absentmindedly as
she continued to scan the room. The apartment was
sumptuous, with papered walls and several pieces of
modish looking furniture; two sets of drawers, a Chinese
lacquered chest, and dressing table by the window. Her
breathing still fast, she strode over to one set of draws
and yanked open the top draw. Her heart beat slowed as
she saw her undergarments and a baby blanket. Again she
stretched out, feeling the soft wool beneath her fingertips
and calming her mind that it was indeed the blanket she

had been left with when she was a baby at the Foundling Hospital.

Soon after she found her spare dress and gloves—all past their best. And finally, the writing case that Miss Drench had gifted her on leaving the charity school. It had been second hand, someone else's name plate on the case, but such a thoughtful gift. Ary was relieved to see it sitting on the side of the dressing table behind some pots and brushes that had been laid out for her to use. She came over to that side of the room, looking at the window, a great sashed affair with four panes abreast and six high, she looked out on the view it afforded. The formal gardens stretched away to the left of the house, and she spotted flowers in bloom in various colours dotting the borders and main beds. She wondered if the Derringer siblings had played in the gardens as children.

Breathing a little easier, Ary turned back to look at the room with a calmer eye. She counted four more empty drawers in the set she had opened, a second cabinet and a deep chest at the end of the bed which were all empty, starved of her non-existent possessions. Duriel Hall was far larger and grander than the widowed Mrs Stanaway's small house in Guildford. And this room was more luxurious than Ary had been given before, or even expected for that matter.

At Mrs Stanaway's house she had slept in one of the smaller bedrooms near to the mistress of the house. She had expected no more at Duriel Hall, but in the short time she had been here, she had been treated like a guest rather than an employee.

Finally, something which caused a spark of excitement caught her eye. She spied a pile of books beside the bed. Striding over to them, forgetting her slow perusal of the rest of the room, she picked the first one up and inhaled the scent.

The aroma of the leather cover, the thick paper, the potential of the world into which she could escape, invaded her nose and mind. That's what reading had been to her. An escape. And when she had told Miss Drench, the severe woman had smiled in a knowing way and replied that reading was an escape in more ways than one.

It had been several years before Ary had realised what her school mistress meant by the cryptic words. Miss Drench had always managed, seemingly miraculously, to pay for books from the circulating library for Ary to read. The older woman had fed Ary's voracious habit, because she had known that such learning could make Ary fit for more than service. With learning she might be a companion or a governess. And now here she was.

Ary glanced down at the rest of the books. No doubt they had been left by mistake. Books were expensive and she could hardly expect any to be given to her, a companion, but perhaps she might flick through them before she returned them to Mr Derringer.

There was a history of Bath and the surrounding area —the one she had already picked up—and still on the table was a copy of the Bible and a novel by Richardson. An eclectic mix. Who had picked these out and left them together? Who did they belong to? Mr Derringer? The thought of him brought to mind those green eyes that had been watching her so intently.

She flicked through the book on Bath for a few minutes, waiting for the memory of those eyes to fade from thought, and soon found her gaze wandering over to the window again. Ordinarily, she would have been content to curl up on the bed with one of these books, but after hours on end in a carriage, she was in no mood to be still. She needed to move and to breathe fresh air.

Curiosity getting the better of her, she left her room, book still in hand, and descended the stairs to the hall once again. She paused, listening to the sounds of the house. Servants' voices murmured far off, there was the faint clattering of pots from some distant kitchen room, and then there was the deep rumble of a man's voice. The latter was nearer, inaudible, but she guessed it must be Mr Derringer. She wondered if they were talking about her.

Her throat contracted as she remembered her awe at the house. Did she amuse them? The poor companion, staring like a frightened lamb at their home. They hadn't appeared to show pity, but it was only a matter of time. She always became the object of pity. Ary pushed away a desire to grimace. How she loathed to be pitied. The desire for fresh air grew acute.

She chose an open door, from which she heard no voices, and left the hall. It brought her into a stone hall, the space opening up to her left and right. She looked up at the high ceiling, gaze running over the sculpted cornices reminiscent of classical Rome. She had read about similar architecture in Inigo Jones' book on Stonehenge where the author had written about Roman and Greek architecture.

Her eyes dropping, she saw the walls were painted in a pale eggshell blue, reflecting the light pouring in from the large windows and double doors straight ahead. Ary walked forwards, her shoes echoing loudly on the marble floor. She rose up onto the balls of her feet to deaden the sound and when she came to the doors she looked out.

The formal gardens stretched out to her left, and she realised she must be directly beneath her bedroom. She was glad the Derringers were not giving her this tour, for she stood transfixed for several minutes, staring at the flowers and shrubs and winding paths, the hedges rising up and then the unsculptured land stretching out beyond. All of this belonged to Duriel Hall.

The desire to be outside grew stronger and she glanced back. No one had found her. She turned to the door and put pressure tentatively on the handle. It turned easily enough and when she pushed it, it opened without protest. A soft breeze fluttered against her skirts and ran across her face. She took in a gusty breath and stepped out, easing the door closed behind her.

Surely she would not be scolded for getting to know the place which would be her home for at least the next six months? She did not trust it would be longer. No place in Ary's life had been permanent and she had learned not to expect it.

The breeze did not abate, and she took another lungful of air feeling its cleansing effect after her long journey cooped up in a carriage. She rolled her shoulders back and stretched her arms to the side as if readying to embrace some invisible being. Her lips lost their firm line in a pleasing curve and her eyes lit with pleasure.

She skipped down the steps of the terrace, realising as she did so, that this was where she had seen someone standing on her approach to the Hall. Mr Derringer? Those green eyes ambushed her thoughts again. He was a handsome man, that Ary would admit, but handsome men in her experience had motives. And those motives— when it came to a companion with no protector—were rarely honourable.

The gravel crunched beneath her boots as she passed a selection of English roses. Their scents were heavily mingling with each other and creating a heady atmosphere. She wondered if Charlotte came here. Perhaps she might accompany her.

A particularly spectacular rose, its blooms large and weighty in beautiful multi-petalled chalices, its hue a soft pink-white, attracted Ary. The breeze moved the flower Ary had bent to smell so she took it between her fingers to steady it.

"Miss Giles?"

The call made Ary start. Her finger and thumb slipped up the rose stem as she jerked her hand away and a thorn pressed into her flesh.

"Blast!"

She snatched her hand back and saw a bright blob of blood oozing from her thumb.

"Miss Giles?"

It was Mrs Higgs, and the woman looked a mite ruffled. She had heard Ary curse. Not a ladylike behaviour for a companion. Neither was sticking your thumb in your mouth as Ary was doing at this moment. Heat bloomed in her cheeks and she wondered how long she would last as a companion to Miss Derringer if her unruly tongue continued to get the better of her.

The housekeeper did no more than raise an eyebrow at Ary.

"I have been looking for you. I could not find you in your rooms when I came to fetch you, Miss Giles. Mr Derringer has said he would like to see you in his study."

The words were a thinly veiled scold. Apparently exploring her new home alone had not been a good idea.

Ary pulled her thumb from her mouth and nodded.

"Yes, Mrs Higgs."

"Come with me, miss." The housekeeper led the way back to the terrace and Ary followed, wondering what sort of reception would await her in Mr Derringer's study, and whether the redoubtable Mrs Higgs would divulge Ary's improper cursing to her new employer.

If she did, Ary had no doubt her engagement with the Derringer's would be cut abruptly short.

CHAPTER 4

William was frowning at the fire when Miss Giles was shown in. He had been informed a short time ago that the new companion was not in her room and Mrs Higgs had gone off in search of her.

"Mr Derringer, here is Miss Giles."

He looked up at the housekeeper's words.

"She was in the gardens," Mrs Higgs added, answering the query on his face.

He looked past her to Miss Giles who waited patiently to be allowed entry into the room. When the housekeeper finally stepped aside he noticed Miss Giles would not catch his eye in greeting. His frown deepened.

It appeared Miss Giles had taken it upon herself to explore. Had she given herself a tour of the house as well? William was not sure whether to admire her forthrightness, or be dismayed at the idea that a woman of uncertain character had been wandering about his family home unattended. He had not made his mind up when Mrs Higgs excused herself and left Miss Giles standing on the threshold.

William observed her. She had fresh colour in her cheeks that had been lacking after her carriage journey. In fact, she looked thoroughly windswept. Her brown hair, with its natural curl, had escaped its pins and a huge lock of it hung over her shoulder. He saw she held a book by her side and recognised it as one of those he had selected for her room.

She was bringing her other hand intermittently up to her mouth. Odd. William could not understand the reason for the movement.

"Miss Giles," he said, realising that once again he had been looking at her for too long. "Will you take a seat?" He gestured to one of the cushioned chairs that sat before his leather-topped desk.

The young woman came further into the room and did as she was bid, taking up residence in one of the chairs, her hand still to her lips. When she finally dropped it, upon catching eyes with William, he observed there was a wariness in her gaze. Even with that look he noticed again how dark those eyes were. He had admired them when he had first seen her this morning and now he could put his finger on why. There was a depth to them, and a keenness, that he could see. He did not think she was some foolish miss.

"You've found the books I see," he said, striking off in an informal tone. He needed to gain her confidence if he was to determine her character. No need to begin with a scolding on her wandering about unattended.

"Oh yes." She held the book up from her lap, offering it to him. "They were left in my room. I can bring the others down too."

He raised a single brow and made no effort to take the book from her.

"Have you read them already?"

"I—no," she admitted, taking in his teasing look, indecision in her own gaze.

"Then you must keep them. That is, if they are to your taste. Otherwise I can find you others. I chose a selection, as I was not sure what you might like."

She looked puzzled. There was a faint crinkle on her otherwise smooth brow, and she didn't immediately say anything. He wished he might read her mind.

"They are for me to read?"

"I don't know what else you would do with a book," William replied. The jovial tone was perhaps a little too informal. "Unless," he said, recalling something and fearing he'd been misled, "you are not a great reader?"

He had assumed from Miss Giles' reaction to the mention of the library earlier that Miss Drench's praise of her charge was true. But the woman could have exaggerated the level of Miss Giles' education and her love of literature. Had he unintentionally highlighted the shortcomings of his sister's new companion?

"I am."

His eyes had dropped from hers, not wanting to cause her any further embarrassment, but they shot back up at that tone. Defiance. He studied her a moment.

"Good," he said at length. "I had it from Mrs Stanaway that you were exceedingly well read," he lied. He could not think of a believable reason why he should have been in correspondence with her old school mistress, so her previous employer would have to do.

She had fallen silent again. He wondered what that look on her face meant. Her brown eyes unreadable, her nose slightly pinched at the sides, her lips pressed together.

"You may consider those books a loan, until you wish to exchange them for others."

Her frown was still present.

"Duriel Hall's library is extensive," he explained. "My grandfather collected most of the volumes. We have a huge number of works on antiquities and the classical world—too many to read in a lifetime—but there are other subjects as well if your interests should be lighter. My sister has added a few novels to the collection."

"I enjoy reading history."

There it was again. A brief spark of challenge in her eyes.

"I was told you had a good level of schooling."

"If you are concerned that my education is not sufficient for being a companion to your sister in Society, then I can assure you I have a thorough understanding of literature, history, and geography, and I am fluent in French and Italian."

That was a surprise.

"You had a thorough governess."

He waited for her to correct him, but she did not. It appeared that even if he set traps for her, she would not fall into them and give away more about herself than she wished.

"Are there other areas you would like to go over?" she asked.

He was certain that if she had been standing she would have placed a hand on her hip. What had he expected? A shy miss? A young woman beaten down by the ills life had thrown her way? Perhaps both.

But Miss Giles was neither. She held his gaze steadily,

her shoulders drawn back, and her chin tipped up a little. No, she was no simpering miss and no despairing woman. Truth be told, William was not sure how he would categorise Miss Giles. She had defied his expectations both in appearance and now in behaviour. But he could not tell whether her forthright attitude was due to a genuine desire to be taken seriously, or because she was a temperamental miss.

"My sister Charlotte—" he said, opting to sit on a nearby chair. Perhaps if he looked less like the master of the house she might be more inclined to soften. "—is due to come out next Season. Our mother died last year and so it has fallen to me to ensure my sister makes her entrance into Society in the best way possible. Without our mother to guide her, I am hardly equipped to lend her the female guidance she requires, which is why I engaged you."

At least... that was half the reason.

"I fear launching Charlotte into the London Season with no experience would be a cruel thing to do. Our mother, you see, intended for her to enjoy some time in Bath in order to get used to being out in Society. That did not happen, as my mother died, and we went into mourning."

"I am sorry," said Miss Giles, her voice much softer than before.

William's eyes flicked from where he had been staring into the middle-distance to the woman's face. While her expression remained closed, he noted her eyes had softened along with her tone.

"Thank you." He shifted, uncrossing and re-crossing his legs. "I wish for Charlotte to have a companion with whom to face Society, and there will be a great deal of it in Bath over the coming weeks. Many of the ton will come here to take the waters before the London Season begins in earnest, and I have secured a number of invitations to gatherings. Bath is the ideal venue in which to introduce Charlotte to Society and I wish you to accompany her."

He noticed her eyes widen a fraction.

"I will be there also, of course, but I cannot provide Charlotte with the female companionship she will no doubt desire."

Was that fear he saw in her eyes? Whatever it was, she quickly covered it.

"Charlotte is the sweetest of sisters and has no knowledge of Society or its"—he did not know how to put it—"harsh realities. I would be grateful, if you would not only provide her with companionship, but also with... your help, where she needs it."

William was sure Miss Giles had noticed Charlotte's stammer earlier. She had not shown it, but he hoped she would understand what he meant.

"Of course," said Miss Giles.

There was sincerity in her voice.

"Oh!"

Miss Giles, whose gaze had fallen from his face to her lap, took on a look of surprised irritation. She snatched up her hand and to William's utter bewilderment she thrust her right thumb into her mouth.

William's brows rose and then knitted together. He wondered for a moment if she was touched in the head.

As if reading his thoughts, Miss Giles' eyes darted to his own, then she yanked her thumb out of her mouth and held it out to him. In explanation, she squeezed it until a red bead of blood appeared.

"I pricked it on a rose."

William's brows unknit and the corner of his mouth pulled upwards. "The perils of exploring alone." He pulled a handkerchief from his pocket and leant forward to offer it to her.

She stared at it, then at him, a look of distrust in her eyes.

"Please," he said, "take it."

Still she waited, sucking her thumb once again.

"I am not scolding you for exploring. This is your home now. But I would prefer to be able to converse with you, if you wouldn't mind. If that is to happen, we must have that thumb removed from your mouth." He offered the handkerchief again, smiling in the hopes she would see it as a peace offering.

After a moment Miss Giles took it tentatively. She wrapped it around her thumb.

"Thank you," she said, bobbing her head.

"You're welcome, but I'm afraid it has not saved your dress." He gestured to where a small patch of blood had soaked into her skirts.

"Dash it," she muttered under her breath.

He found himself grinning at the improper language. Unfortunately, at that moment she looked up and caught his expression. He wiped it from his face immediately.

"Perhaps you would like to change your dress and then meet me and my sister in the hall?" He rose from his chair. "If you do not need to rest, and are so keen on exploring, then we shall have to show you the Hall. Clearly you cannot be trusted to traverse it alone."

He had meant it as a joke, but it did not land as such. He caught a look first of annoyance and then of embarrassment on Miss Giles' face.

She rose, murmuring an apology for going into the gardens without permission, and before he could tell her that he had not meant it as a scold, she left. He perched himself on his desk once again and ran a hand over his face.

What had he learned? She was well-educated, clearly. She was curious, otherwise she wouldn't have gone off exploring on her own. And she was defiant. Some might consider that last trait a negative, but William was undecided. It showed him that, after all she had endured, her spirit had not been broken.

No, it was not a negative trait to William. Rather, he found himself admiring her for it. But it was too early to tell if she was a woman of character. He needed more time to get to know her before he revealed his hand.

CHAPTER 5

*A*ry counted to one hundred in her room. Gauging that would be about the time taken to change her dress, she rose. Drawing her shoulders back she left her room and came back down the stairs hoping that Mr Derringer would not notice that she had not changed. She would have to soak the stain tonight. Perhaps Mrs Higgs had some remedy.

She still held Mr Derringer's handkerchief around her thumb, though the bleeding had stopped. She glanced down at it as she walked. No man had offered her his handkerchief before, but she had hesitated to take it. Miss Drench had told her about unscrupulous masters seducing their servants. Mr Derringer was still an unknown quantity, no matter how kind his eyes or his playful attempts to put her at ease.

As she rounded the final bend in the stairs, she pushed the stain behind a pleat of her dress and raised her chin. Mr Derringer was waiting for her at the bottom, with Charlotte standing beside him. Ary was thrown off-balance by her employer's direct stare.

"You did not change," he said when she reached the bottom step.

She halted, glancing between Charlotte and Mr Derringer. The latter looked genuinely puzzled.

Keeping her eyes on his, she replied, "I only have one other dress, and it is in need of laundering." She said the words frankly and without the least note of shame. Ary might feel the embarrassment keenly, but that did not mean she had to show it.

"Oh d-dear," Charlotte said, blushing.

"Hmm," Mr Derringer murmured, his gaze having drifted to a space just above Ary's head, "that will not do."

The embarrassment Ary had been keeping under control threatened to overwhelm her, and splashed her cheeks with crimson. It was not her fault she was poor. Defiant anger rose within her, warring against the tide of embarrassment.

"We shall have to arrange a full wardrobe for you," he carried on, answering the question that sprang up in Ary's mind before she could voice it, "which we shall cover the cost of aside from your wages, of course. I'm sure my sister will be delighted to spend more time at the modiste, wouldn't you, Lottie?"

Charlotte returned his grin and batted his arm playfully.

"W-would you l-like that?" Charlotte asked, turning back to Ary.

Ary looked between the brother and sister, her embarrassment ebbing in the face of surprise. They wished to purchase an entire wardrobe for her? She had never known such generosity. This couldn't be right. Where was the catch?

"In the meantime you may borrow a dress from Lottie. She has far too many as it is."

"That is because you are too soft with me brother," Charlotte replied, her stammer gone in the face of her brother's funning. "But of course you may. William told me about the rose thorn." Charlotte smiled at her, nodding her head encouragingly.

Ary did not immediately reply, unsure what to make of the situation. Surely they did not mean it—for her to be taken to a modiste and have dresses made? But there was no wicked amusement in their eyes. No desire to deceive her. They were in earnest.

"I could not—"

"I should have thought of it before," Mr Derringer said, cutting her off. "I apologise." He inclined his head to her.

He was saying sorry? What was this?

"I doubt being a companion to Mrs Stanaway occasioned the need for an extensive wardrobe. From what I know she was not one for Society."

It was true. Her engagement with Mrs Stanaway had been largely to keep her company at her home. There was the occasional caller, but in those times Ary would sit in the corner of the morning room and maintain a silent presence while her employer chatted with her elderly friends.

A handful of times they had gone to a local gathering. It was there Ary had learned how to conduct herself in Society. She had watched and observed and learned the way of things. But those occasions were hardly the societal events she would be expected to attend with Mr and Miss Derringer.

"I..." she trailed off, unsure of the appropriate response.

"Lottie, will you go with Miss Giles and find her a suitable dress? You may both meet me in the drawing room when you're ready."

Mr Derringer gave Ary a reassuring smile and she was struck by his handsomeness.

"Oh yes, come with me. I'm sure to have something that will s-suit," Charlotte said, more confident than before.

Ary was carried along on their logic and soon found herself in Charlotte's room, gazing at more dresses than she had ever seen before. Charlotte's maid helped Ary to change out of her dress, while her mistress sat on the edge of her bed smiling at Ary.

"He's the most thoughtful brother," Charlotte said. As she did, she pulled a silk *robe à la française* from where she had thrown a series of dresses on the bed, and offered it up to Ary. "Do you l-like this one?"

It was the most beautiful dress Ary had ever been offered.

"It looks very fine," she said, uncertainly.

"Oh, I know it is not in the latest s-style," Charlotte replied apologetically. "You may have a *robe à l'anglaise* if you prefer a fitted back. I realise a sacque gown is a bit formal for day wear, but I think the orange will set off your eyes and h-hair w-wonderfully."

Ary did not correct her misapprehension. She hardly knew how to voice her thoughts—that this dress was meant for a lady of quality, not someone like Ary.

"I am happy to wear something plainer."

"Nonsense," the elderly maid said in a motherly

fashion. "Miss Derringer's right. The colour will become you very well with your hair dark as it is."

Ary acquiesced reluctantly, stepping into the matching petticoat first and allowing the maid to tie it around her waist. Next came the gown. The maid settled it around Ary's shoulders, making an approving noise as she stepped back to check it was sitting right, before deftly pinning the stomacher in place.

"Pretty as a picture, miss."

Ary turned to the mirror, inexplicably nervous. As soon as she saw herself she realised the maid and Miss Derringer had been right. The colour of the dress, echoing the peel of a Seville orange, set off the darkness of Ary's unpowdered hair and brown eyes.

"Lovely," Charlotte said, standing up from the bed. "Now, shall we get back to William? I think you are going to like the Hall."

Ary did not doubt it. What she did doubt, was whether the owners of the Hall would still be so kind to her if they knew the truth.

ARY DID LIKE THE HALL. Not for its grandness, its many rooms or its appealing setting. Rather, she was fascinated by the many exotic objects they passed by—on the tables, hanging from the walls, or kept in cabinets. Mr Derringer explained his father had been on the Grand Tour in his youth and that his travels had extended to several years after marrying their Italian mother. It had led to an impressive collection of artefacts and pieces of art.

Ary marvelled at a pair of terrestrial and celestial globes. Then there were the Renaissance triptychs picked up in Florence, and the ebony and ivory crossbow from some bygone age. Finally there was an illuminated manuscript in a cabinet and next to it lay a history of the Roman empire from the last century.

Ary did her best not to stare for too long, but twice she caught Mr Derringer's eyes on her.

They stopped in the drawing room that looked over the gardens she had escaped into earlier.

Mr Derringer was pulled aside by a servant leaving Ary and Charlotte free to talk.

"D-do you like the Hall?" asked Charlotte, vulnerability marking her expression.

"Yes. It is very beautiful."

"Oh g-good, I'm glad."

Ary's heart squeezed for the girl who could not help but stammer when speaking to her. She wished to tell Charlotte that she need not worry about it, that Ary was not judging her for it, but she knew drawing attention to it would not help. She had known a boy with a similar stammer at the charity school, and the only thing that had helped was to ignore it. That and singing. Perhaps Ary could contrive a way for them to spend time singing together. If only she knew how to play the pianoforte.

"I am s-so g-glad you are h-here."

The stammer was growing worse.

"I know William says I m-must go out in S-Society. I have been d-dreading doing it a-alone."

Ary's heart compressed harder. The last sentiment was one she could empathise with so entirely. If she had known the girl better, she might have taken Charlotte's hand.

"I shall be with you," she replied with conviction.

Her mind took a pause. She was unwise to commit so soon when she did not know these people. She must remember to guard her heart, for things always changed, and what was pleasant one day might be something she must leave the next. That was why she understood Charlotte's feelings so entirely. Ary had always been alone. The difference was that Charlotte had a brother. Ary had no one, and once her job here was done, she would be alone again.

"I apologise," said Mr Derringer, rejoining them. "It appears the rout at Lord and Lady Mires is to go ahead as Lady Amelia has recovered from her cold. We can attend this Friday if you both wish it?"

"I should like to see Amelia again," Charlotte responded immediately, her stammer dropping when she addressed her brother.

"Good. And Miss Giles, will you be sufficiently recovered from your journey for your first engagement?"

Apparently Ary was to be constantly surprised today. First the offer of a wardrobe, then borrowing this silk dress, and now she was asked if she would be well-rested enough to attend a party.

"Yes, Mr Derringer, of course."

"Good—right, the gardens are next. Lottie, keep a close eye on your companion, she has been attacked by our roses once today. We can't have her wandering off unattended and succumbing to our treacherous gardens again."

CHAPTER 6

The Mires' rout came around far quicker than Ary wished. By the time Friday arrived she hated to admit she was nervous. At least, she mused while having her hair dressed by Miss Derringer's maid, Charlotte was truly as kind as she had at first appeared. Ary steeled herself for the task at hand and when her hair was dressed, she rose and went downstairs.

As she came into the hall she saw Mr Derringer waiting by the entrance.

"Miss Giles." He bowed towards her, and she noticed when he rose that he was giving her an appraising look.

She raised her chin a little, but did not manage to keep his gaze for long. She did not wish to be told she looked the fool she felt. A foundling child dressed up as a lady. She had not even looked at herself in the mirror on leaving her room.

"You look lovely this evening, Miss Giles," said Mr Derringer, his voice lower than usual.

She glanced over at him and saw, to her surprise, a genuineness in his eyes. Had he really meant that?

"Th-thank you," she replied, irritated at herself for stammering.

She drew her shoulders back in an effort to regain some control, but did not meet his eyes again. She could not work Mr Derringer out. After her initial interview with him, he had spoken to her several times over dinner, asking how she was getting on with the books he had lent her.

While the questions were innocuous enough, he had a way of looking at her that made her feel as though she were under some kind of examination. It was not with desire, as some men had looked at her in the past, but with a keenness that brought up her guard.

"Have you attended a rout before?" he asked, raising a questioning brow.

The query forced Ary to look at him again. She did not wish to appear rude. Her heart beat a little faster as she took in his appearance. He was wearing a finely cut silk suit of deep green. The jacket was cut away at the sides with gold embroidery along its edges. Her gaze took in his broad shoulders and the lace cravat at his neck, an emerald winking at her from its folds and bringing out the green of his eyes.

His hair was lightly powdered and held back with a matching green ribbon, but there was no powder or patch on his face. His skin was clear and lightly tanned from going about the estate, as she had learned he spent most of his time doing. And she noted the freshly shaved line of his strong jaw.

Mr Derringer was handsome—she had recognised that when she had first met him and again when he had been kind to her—but this evening that fact was magnified.

"Miss Giles?"

"No," she said hurriedly, blushing as she realised she had been too busy admiring him to think to answer.

He looked as though he expected more, but she did not oblige him. His questions seemed intent on piercing the veil of her past, which she would rather not lift. She had no desire to be judged. No wish for him to form opinions about her based on her past rather than her present actions. The question brought back the guards that she hid the truth behind. A charming smile and green eyes were not enough to engage her trust.

"W-William." Charlotte's voice came from the foot of the stairs and Ary turned towards it.

Out of the corner of her eye, she noticed Mr Derringer's gaze stayed on her, a light frown knitting his brow.

"I-I'm not sure ab-bout this d-dress," said Charlotte, pressing a hand to her bodice.

Mr Derringer came forward, his wooden heels clipping on the marble floor.

"Nonsense, sister, you look very fine indeed. Didn't you choose the fabric?" Her brother's pragmatic words did little to help.

Ary noted that they had the opposite effect.

"Oh-oh, I know. The c-colour is—it is—so b-bright."

"Well, it is too late to worry over it now, and I tell you, you look beautiful, sister," said Mr Derringer.

Charlotte looked down at her dress and then back up at her brother, unconvinced.

"Yellow is a colour that shows off your fair skin, Miss Derringer," said Ary, stepping forward and taking Charlotte's hand onto her arm. "And the style shows off your figure to great advantage." She opted for a soft and coaxing tone, the antithesis of Mr Derringer's. "You have nothing to fear. You will be very well-received in such a dress."

"D-do you think so?" asked Charlotte, and then nodded as she took her cloak from a waiting servant. "Y-yes, you're probably right."

Ary could feel Mr Derringer's presence close behind them as she took Charlotte on her arm again and headed for the door.

"And remember," said Ary as they stepped out onto the drive together, "I shall be with you all evening. Any time you feel uncertain you may squeeze my hand and I will take us off to some quiet place where you may catch your breath."

Charlotte bestowed a grateful smile on Ary and then was handed up into the waiting carriage.

Ary waited for the servant to turn back for her, but she felt a hand take her own before they could.

"Thank you," Mr Derringer murmured as he drew her forward and handed her up into the carriage.

She caught an intense look in those green eyes of his and found herself looking away. When he climbed in after her and settled opposite, she risked another glance in his direction, but his features were swallowed up by the carriage's dark interior and she was left none the wiser as to his thoughts.

She was merely doing the job she had been hired for, yet there had been such sincere thankfulness in his gaze it surprised her. The feeling that she was helping Charlotte was a good one, but she knew she could not get too attached—not to her charge or to her employer. Her time here was finite, and allowing her feelings to grow would expose her to pain in the end.

Turning to the window, she watched the shadows of trees pass by, and allowed the silence to rebuild the walls around her heart. High and wide they were. They would protect her. They must. A pair of kind green eyes could not pierce them... could they?

CHAPTER 7

The kindness with which Miss Giles had assuaged his sister's nerves impressed William. He watched her profile in the carriage, becoming clearer as they made progress into the Bath streets. She had been glued to that window since entering the vehicle. The only times she had turned from the view was to answer his sister. It would have been natural for her to glance in his direction as she did so, for she sat opposite him, but she had not.

In fact, he was fairly certain she was avoiding looking at him altogether. Was he such an ogre to her? Had he not thanked her for what she had done? Most women would be tittering and fawning over such compliments.

When they arrived at the Mires' residence in Great Pultney Street, William exited the carriage first, turning to hand down Charlotte and then Miss Giles. The latter continued to avoid his gaze and was quick to take her hand back once she had alighted.

"Here we are—your first engagement, Lottie,"

William said, excitement for his sister in his voice. "Come."

He offered an arm to each lady. Charlotte took one readily, but Miss Giles failed to take the other. She stood wide-eyed, staring up at the grand classical façade of the Mires' house.

"You have nothing to fear," William whispered down to her.

Her eyes darted to his face, and then to his offered arm. She finally took it, an indecipherable look in her eyes, and they ascended the steps to the house together.

On entering the residence William felt Ary's hand tighten on his arm despite his reassurances. The house was no less impressive inside as it was outside. The entrance hall was all gilt, carved wood, and rich furnishings. They passed multiple footmen on their way to the stairs, all stood to attention in matching livery. And then there were the attendees—silks and brocades, lace and powdered hair, diamonds and emeralds.

When William looked down at Ary, he saw her chin was raised in that way of hers. He had thought it defiance before, but perhaps it was fear.

"Mr Derringer, always a pleasure," said Lord Mires, the plain man all generous smiles.

"Lord Mires." William released his sister and Miss Giles to shake his Lordship's hand. "I trust you are enjoying the book I lent you?"

"Indeed, my boy. Roman Bath is a particular fascination of mine and I'd willingly talk to you about it all night, but we are being impolite to the two beautiful ladies you have with you this evening. Wife, take a look at young Miss Derringer, and, ah…"

William bowed towards Lady Mires who turned to join them.

"Your Ladyship, my sister, Miss Derringer, you know, and may I present her companion, Miss Giles?"

William held out a hand for Miss Giles to come forward, and she did so with a great deal of poise, curtseying gracefully and thanking Lady Mires for her hospitality. He felt unrealised tension in his shoulders dissipate. He had been more concerned about whether Ary would be able to conduct herself properly in Society than he had thought.

"You're welcome, my child. And Miss Derringer, you'll find Amelia somewhere in one of these rooms."

"Causing a ruckus, no doubt," said Lord Mires, his smile belying any hint of reprimand. "Always loud and laughing, that girl. Takes after her mother."

"Th-thank you, Lady Mires," Charlotte replied, colouring slightly at Lord Mire's jibe at his wife.

They exchanged a few more pleasantries and then took their leave to join the rest of the party.

"D-do you think they n-noticed my stutter?" Charlotte whispered to Miss Giles.

William walked behind them, and saw Miss Giles squeeze his sister's hand. "You spoke very well. Don't be afraid to take your time over your words this evening. And you can always try humming for a moment before you start. I used to know a little boy who struggled with his speech. He hummed before he spoke, and it did him a great deal of good."

That was the first time she had freely offered anything up about her past. Miss Giles said something else that William did not catch. Steering them towards the drinks table, he procured a glass of punch for each lady before getting his own.

"Ary says—that is, M-Miss Giles—that I should speak slowly if I wish," Charlotte began dragging out her words as she spoke to her brother, "to help with my stammer. She says I am pretty enough for others to wait on my words."

"Did she, indeed?" William asked, one brow rising and a half-smile hovering on his lips. "Wise words from Miss Giles."

He was rewarded with a brief smile from the woman in question. Another surprise. She had not smiled at him before, her gaze always firm, her expression passive. Could he hope that she was finally opening up? Miss Giles took a sip of her drink and then avoided his gaze. Perhaps not.

"Lottie!" came a cry from halfway across the room.

William had no trouble recognising the seventeen year-old, fresh-faced girl almost running towards them, silk dress billowing, curled hair bobbing.

"Amelia!" Charlotte replied, a brilliant smile breaking out across her features as she stretched out her hands to the girl. Lady Amelia took them, grinning at her friend.

"Isn't it splendid? I told you Mama and Papa had promised me a great crush for my first societal event. It's bigger than the one Louise had," said Lady Amelia, referring to her elder sister. "I swear it and—oh! How rude of me. Your brother is here."

The energetic girl had whirled around and dropped into a poorly executed curtsey when she realised William was there. Then she took in Miss Giles and her mouth formed a perfect circle. "And?"

"Lady Amelia, may I present Miss Giles—companion to my sister?"

Miss Giles curtseyed gracefully again. "A pleasure to meet you, Lady Amelia."

"Oh yes, a pleasure. Lottie told me you were arriving. I had it in my head that you would be a ghastly old woman—but she is not, is she?"

"No," William said with more certainty than he intended. "She is not."

He felt Miss Giles' eyes upon him, but he chose not to return the look.

"It is a pleasure. She is so pretty, is she not, Lottie? Anyway"—Lady Amelia carried on without pausing for breath—"shall I show you the games mama and papa have allowed in the other room? May I steal Lottie?"

"You may," said William, a benevolent smile on his face.

The two women linked arms and turned to leave. Miss Giles made to follow, but William stopped her.

"I believe they will be safe lending each other countenance," he said, smiling at her. "And I think you may appreciate the respite, for there is plenty more of this youthful excitement in store for us tonight."

Miss Giles looked after the young women, threading their way through the crowd, and then back at him. There was uncertainty in her eyes. He willed her to stay.

William had seen a glimpse of her true character just now, when she was speaking to Charlotte, and he desired to see more. Exhaling his satisfaction when she agreed to stay, he refilled her punch glass and handed it back to her, hoping that he might glimpse again the woman beneath the passive mask.

He denied that her dark eyes and pleasing lips had

anything to do with wanting to get to know her better. No. It was purely so that he might assess her character before playing his hand. Yes, that was it. He had brought her to Duriel Hall for a purpose and he must see it through. He had made a promise, and he intended to keep it.

CHAPTER 8

"I have been meaning to ask," said Mr Derringer.

Ary watched him pause to take a sip of punch.

"Is your thumb healed from its thorny encounter?"

Why had he kept her back from going with his sister? No employer usually advocated giving his servant's a break while on duty.

"Yes," Ary replied, after a moment's hesitation. "Thank you."

"Good," replied Mr Derringer, giving a nod of satisfaction. "I must thank you for being so kind to my sister."

Ary's brows rose a fraction. "I believe that is the job you hired me for, is it not?"

"Yes," he conceded. "But you show more care than most."

He had that look of curiosity in his eyes again, that one which made her feel as though he were examining and measuring her. Her guard went up involuntarily.

"I cannot attest to that."

He looked put out at her abrupt words. Good. He was piercing her guard and she didn't like it. He must stay firmly on the other side of her walls.

"I can." When he spoke his tone was firm. "Not everyone would say such kind words to Charlotte. There were plenty of governesses who tried to discipline the stammer out of my sister."

"And how successful were they?" asked Ary, her chin rising and her gaze direct.

She had watched plenty of school teachers beat the children in the charity school. The practice was barbaric and pointless in her opinion.

To her surprise, Mr Derringer smiled, or was it grinned?

"Precisely."

He raised his glass to her in a mock salute and she felt an unbidden tug at each corner of her mouth.

"You seem to understand her affliction better than most—you said you knew a young boy with a stammer —was that true?"

He had been eavesdropping. Ary cursed inwardly for sharing anything about her past with the Derringers.

"I am not in the habit of lying."

The rude words had the opposite effect to that which she intended. She had hoped to drive away any interest he had in conversing with her, but instead, when she caught his gaze she saw amusement there.

"The second time I am put in my place by Miss Giles. First she is a scholar, and now a truth-teller. I should stop putting my foot in my mouth when I'm conversing with you."

Again she felt the tug at the corner of her mouth and

an unwanted second smile rolled out over her lips before she could halt it.

When Mr Derringer saw her expression an answering smile lit his own face. The action caused her cheeks to flush. What was she about, smiling at her employer and allowing him to smile back at her? This was becoming far too intimate a conversation. She wiped the smile from her face.

"Will you tell me about the boy?" Mr Derringer asked.

No matter how much she was trying to put him off, he seemed intent on continuing the conversation.

"He stammered, but he learned to overcome it."

Mr Derringer exhaled audibly, and she saw a muscle in the side of his jaw flex.

"Will you tell me more?" he asked. "It would be good to know if the humming worked."

"It did, after a time."

He exhaled loudly again and this time she was sure he was annoyed. At what? Her unwillingness to converse on a deeper level? Why should that bother him? No other man had been interested in Ary's conversation. No. They had been interested in something else entirely.

There was something about the look in his eyes, so genuinely curious, and the care he was showing for his sister, that made Ary lower her defences.

"He developed the stammer after he had been severely beaten. I believe the resulting nervousness caused his speech issues. Whenever he was scolded, even verbally, after that beating, his stammering would worsen. I determined that though a previous schoolmaster had wished to cane it out of the boy, it would be far better to focus on affirming him, to try and sooth his nerves rather than fraying them. He enjoyed singing in the parish choir, and I noticed that he never stuttered when he sang, so I encouraged him to sing his words to me. Eventually humming had the same effect. He never overcame the stammer entirely, but it was lessened."

The look of intense interest in Mr Derringer's face gave Ary a sense of importance she had hitherto not felt in her short life. Here was a gentleman, who knew far greater persons than her, and yet he was choosing to converse with his sister's new companion and listen to what she had to say. Perhaps she had been wrong to hold him at arm's length. Perhaps he was a man of character.

"And how did you come across this boy?"

Ary felt suddenly exposed by her own words. Why had she spoken so freely?

He seemed about to repeat his question when someone hailed him from across the room.

"I thought that was you, Derringer!"

The intimacy which had sprung up between Ary and Mr Derringer dissipated, and she realised just how rapidly she had let her guard down. In a moment, it was back up again.

"Mr Roberts," Mr Derringer called.

A lady and gentleman were approaching. The latter was a tall, broad man with brown eyes—someone whom Ary supposed would be called handsome by most. But there was a flush to his cheek, which she immediately recognised as drink, and it set her teeth on edge.

"Derringer, dear man. Good to see you." The burly man took Mr Derringer's hand and pumped it furiously.

"Miss Sade." Mr Derringer bowed to the lady.

The woman was very beautiful. She was tall and slender, dressed in a pink *robe à la française* worn over a heavily trimmed white petticoat. She curtseyed prettily to Mr Derringer, a coquettish look in her eyes as she batted her lashes in his direction.

While Ary had to own the dress was pretty, the tasselled sash woven around the woman's waist, and the matching turban she wore atop a very high coiffure, were somewhat comical. Charlotte had shown Ary fashion plates with such styles, but in truth, Ary had thought them a joke in their fancifulness. Apparently not.

"May I present Miss Giles, my sister's companion?" Mr Derringer moved back to allow Ary access to the circle.

She curtseyed, trying her best to do so calmly, though she felt the appraising eyes of both newcomers burning into her. As she inclined her head, she became aware of the slightly overlarge dress she wore. While the Derringers had ordered several day and evening dresses for Ary from the dressmaker earlier in the week, none had been ready for this evening, and so she was wearing one of Charlotte's hand-me-downs. Ary had felt pretty after putting it on, but now, before a lady in Society, she could not help but feel a little dowdy.

"A pleasure," Mr Roberts purred, reaching out to take up Ary's hand, which she had not offered, and breathing a kiss over its gloved back. "Quite a beauty."

It took all of Ary's self-control not to snatch her hand back.

"Oh yes, quite a countrified girl, are you not?" Miss Sade asked, but it really wasn't a question that required an answer.

In fact, Ary was fairly certain, it wasn't a question at all. It was an insult. She refrained from her desire to say she had never been a country girl. It would only lead to questions, and she hardly wished to admit she came from London, from the Foundling Hospital, no less.

"You are too kind," Ary murmured, keeping her eyes low.

"What a sweet companion for your darling sister," Miss Sade said, turning sultry eyes on Mr Derringer.

It had not occurred to Ary, until this moment, that Mr Derringer was likely a desirable bachelor in this neighbourhood. After all, he commanded a fair estate and as far as she knew had no fixed love interest. It was growing patently clear that Miss Sade wished to change that.

"Mr Roberts clearly thinks so," Miss Sade said, tittering behind her fan, flicking her eyes to where the fawning man still held Ary's hand.

"Have you been hiding this gem away from me, Derringer?"

"No such thing," Mr Derringer said.

Ary could have sworn her employer's smile looked a little forced.

"She has only this week arrived in Bath. But perhaps I might ask you to release her hand? She did injure it in the garden only a few days since."

Mr Roberts gave up her hand immediately, bowing gallantly and apologising if he caused her any excessive pain. The only pain she felt was that of embarrassment at his clear flirtation.

"Gardening? Oh my." Miss Sade fanned herself as if to keep away the thought of menial labour. "I didn't realise companions were also required to garden."

"Miss Giles has many accomplishments," Mr Derringer replied.

Ary glanced at him. Was he... funning?

"She took her life in her own hands," Mr Derringer carried on, the gleam in his eye only appearing when he looked at Ary, "when she engaged with the roses."

"Oh, I do so love the roses at Duriel Hall," said Miss Sade, not in the least interested in the origins of Ary's injury, nor acknowledging whatever was passing between Mr Derringer and his sister's companion. "I should like to see them again before their blooms have gone."

"I am sure the rose was just jealous of your beauty, Miss Giles," said Mr Roberts, overriding Miss Sade's transparent attempt to gain an invitation to the Hall.

Ary opted for silence.

"Quiet thing, aren't you?" Mr Roberts asked after a few moments.

Apparently silence was not acceptable. She looked at Mr Derringer, who was observing her, and then at Miss Sade. Ary was a representative of the Derringer household. It would not do for her to appear rude.

"I apologise," she said, thinking quickly of something to say. "I was just admiring Miss Sade's dress."

The woman in question, who had been looking with undisguised displeasure at Ary, transformed into a self-deprecating figure. She wafted her fan, shaking her head in the perfect act of not wanting compliments. Her other hand drifted casually over her garb, as if to guide the party to admire her.

"You are too kind."

"I wondered," said Ary, wishing to prolong the conversational diversion, "if perhaps the inspiration for your dress was taken from the *Arabian Nights' Entertainment.*"

Ary had thought of the book when she had first seen

Charlotte's fashion plates. She had read it last year and Miss Sade's garb seemed in keeping.

"Oh my, but aren't you sweet in your country ways! No, my child."

Miss Sade, Ary was almost certain, was the same age as herself.

"It is a *robe à la turque*. Inspired by quite a different place." Miss Sade was tittering again, looking to Mr Roberts who guffawed on her command.

Ary's chin came up. Thankfully, before she could buckle under the temptation to speak her mind, Miss Sade turned the conversation.

"You are good to keep Miss Giles company, Mr Derringer. Tell me, are the gardens looking as magnificent as they did last year?"

Mr Derringer answered her questions, and it was soon obvious that Ary and Mr Roberts were surplus to the conversation. In one of the brief moments that Miss Sade paused to draw breath, Ary made her excuses to leave.

"But I hope you will not go far," said Mr Roberts, warmth in his eyes. "I should like to get better acquainted with you, Miss Giles."

Ary sought refuge in silence once again, only nodding and trying her best to ignore Mr Roberts' leering gaze as she went off to find Charlotte. Once she was away from the group, she could breathe again.

She wove through the crowds keeping an eye out for Charlotte. She had hoped to be as invisible in this job as she had been serving Mrs Stanaway. But this was no engagement to an elderly widow. No, she was in Society now. She would be observed and scrutinised and found wanting. Or worse, viewed as an exotic object and drawing the kind of attention she would do well to avoid.

Already she had felt the keenness of Miss Sade's judgement, and that was without knowing Ary's past. Even Mr Roberts' overt friendliness would be worsened should he find out that Ary had no family to protect her.

Where Mr Derringer had slowly drawn down her guard and caused her to share something of herself, she recognised weakness. Ary needed to protect herself. It would bring shame not only on her, but on Charlotte, if her past was found out. For herself it did not matter, but she had no wish to harm a girl who appeared so kind and generous.

Every step through the crowded rooms of Lord and Lady Mires' establishment put a stone back in the walls of Ary's defences until finally, as she came upon Charlotte, she was fully on her guard again.

They must never find out she was a foundling child.

CHAPTER 9

William watched Miss Giles disappear into the crowds with only half an ear on what Miss Sade was saying. He had expected Miss Giles to be... well, what *had* he expected? Most women of his acquaintance the same age were either painfully shy or far too talkative. An example of the latter was currently talking his ear off.

But Miss Giles could be assigned to neither camp. She was quiet, yes, but not shy. Her dark eyes were wary, and she was careful in what she said. That made her a mystery.

"Where did you find the country girl?" Miss Sade asked, bringing William's attention back to her.

The lady was looking at him with a hint of peevishness, and he realised his conversational partner had found him out. He had *not* been listening.

"She came on recommendation."

"Oh? I've not heard of her. She was with no one of consequence before?"

William smiled. Miss Sade returned the expression, not realising his was one of polite irritation, not pleasure.

"A Mrs Stanaway. I doubt you would know her. She was a widowed friend of my mother's."

"Stanaway." Miss Sade shut her fan and tapped it to her chin.

William was sure the action was not natural. He had been in Society long enough to recognise the coquettish ways of the young ladies on the lookout for a husband. Until his sister was settled, however, he had no wish to think of marriage.

Besides, Miss Sade was not the sort of woman he could think of marrying. He held no desire to court a woman who delighted in putting others down and who had nothing more between her ears than silk and lace.

"I believe my mother also knew a Mrs Stanaway."

William tensed. He should not have revealed the name.

"Do you suppose Miss Giles may be lacking a little education?"

William needn't have worried. Miss Sade was already on to her next put down.

"I know you spoke of her accomplishments, but her comment on my dress, well..." Miss Sade trailed off, her eyes wide and her fan at the corner of her mouth as she smiled appealingly.

"Ah yes, the *Arabian Nights' Entertainment*. I think you'll find, Miss Sade, that Miss Giles was referring to the style of dress which has been adopted across Arabia and thence to the Ottoman empire." He could see he was losing Miss Sade. "So you see," he continued, not without a small amount of satisfaction, "while you thought you were talking at cross-purposes, Miss Giles was correct in what she said. A *robe à la turque* is one and the same as Arabian dress."

Vexation flashed across Miss Sade's countenance, but she covered it quickly.

"I declare," she said, flicking her fan open and wafting herself, "she must be a bluestocking knowing such things. I can't imagine spending so much time reading."

No, William thought, smiling. He was sure Miss Sade did not spend half as much time reading as Miss Giles.

At that moment Miss Sade's mother came to join them. Mr Derringer bowed and greeted her politely.

"Mr Derringer, you will forgive me—but who is that woman?" The middle-aged lady pointed a plump finger to where Miss Giles had just come back into the ballroom with Charlotte and Amelia.

"That is Miss Giles, companion to my sister."

"Companion..." Mrs Sade murmured thoughtfully. "Tell me, is she a relation of yours?" She turned her eyes on William. "She looks familiar to me."

"No." The hairs on the back of William's neck were rising again. "Miss Giles is not a relation."

"She was companion to Mrs Stanaway before, Mama. I seem to remember you knowing a Mrs Stanaway?"

"Oh yes," Mrs Sade replied. "That does ring a bell. She was friends with your mother, was she not, Mr Derringer?"

"Yes." William's chest tightened. How was it possible she recognised Miss Giles? It had been more than twenty years.

"She is causing quite the stir, Mama," said Miss Sade,

the colour of jealousy not becoming her. "First Mr Roberts is taken with her, and now you."

"I feel I know her—as though I've met her before," said Mrs Sade, more to herself than the others.

"Perhaps you saw her when she was companion to Mrs Stanaway?" William offered, using the piece of truth he had unwittingly allowed to pass his lips, to try and deter Mrs Sade from the path of truth.

"Perhaps." Mrs Sade did not appear convinced. "Though truth be told, I cannot remember the last time I saw the lady before she died. She was so out of sorts after Mr Stanaway passed away."

"Will you stare at her all night, Mama, or join in my conversation with Mr Derringer?" Miss Sade goaded. She took her mother's hand onto her arm and turned her to face them so she could no longer see Miss Giles.

"That's enough of your spice, child," Mrs Sade replied tartly. "And as for you Mr Derringer, when will you call on us again?"

William noted the imperious tones—far more characteristic of Mrs Sade's conversation—had returned.

"It has been too long since you and your lovely sister graced us with your presence on a morning call."

"My apologies, madam," said William, not wishing in the least for the offered engagement. "I am sure we will call on you soon, now that Charlotte is out in Society."

"Tomorrow would do well, would it not Eliza?"

William flexed his jaw, displeased with the way the woman had manoeuvred him, but unable to decline given his sister's need to be out in Society. "I'm sure my sister would be delighted. Now if you will excuse me, I should like to find Charlotte and see how she goes on."

Before Miss Sade could wheedle her way onto his

arm, he took his leave. Walking through the throng, he considered it a fortunate escape that Mrs Sade had not worked out who Miss Giles was.

William had known there were many in Society who would have been contemporaries of Miss Giles' mother —Mrs Sade being one of them—but it had never occurred to him that Miss Giles might be recognised. He had never met her mother or seen her likeness and therefore had not considered that Miss Giles might bear a striking resemblance to her mother. Striking enough that someone might recognise her.

Traversing the main room and finding no sign of his sister or Miss Giles, he headed for the card room where Amelia had been taking them earlier. They were likely back there enjoying the entertainment.

He found the room crowded. All the tables were occupied, the loudest one containing all the young people, who were energetically either playing or observing the game.

William caught sight of his sister giggling with Lady Amelia. They were standing behind one of the young men at play. Lady Amelia pointed at the man's cards and then whispered something to Charlotte. Both girls set to giggling again.

"Oh, come now!" cried the young man, his chin still rounded by youth. "I am being outed by these two ladies. I have no chance."

"S-sorry, Mr Latham," Charlotte stammered, a smile still on her lips.

"S-sorry won't cut it if I lose this hand," Mr Latham mimicked, huffing at the cards in his grasp.

Charlotte's smile vanished, red stealing up her cheeks.

"We meant nothing by it, you frightful man," Lady Amelia said with asperity. "You have a very fine hand, Mr Latham, and so I tell all your competitors."

William saw that Lady Amelia's sharp answer had done little to assuage his sister's embarrassment. His chest tightened at the sight of Charlotte's discomfort.

"Perhaps I do," Mr Latham conceded, a sly smile licking across his lips. "But the element of surprise has been lost, and I need my bet to pay for a horse out of Viscount Arleigh's stud. No amount of s-sorry will bring my two hundred pounds back if I lose it."

Where was Miss Giles? William searched the crowds for a sign of her. He felt a rising ire at her absence. He had told the new companion that Charlotte was not used to Society. This was exactly the sort of situation he had wanted Miss Giles to protect his sister from.

"Perhaps"—a voice came from somewhere behind William's sister and Miss Giles materialised at Charlotte's elbow—"the fault lies with you—Mr Latham, was it?"

There was something authoritative in Miss Giles' calm voice. William wondered if that was the way she had spoken to errant young boys at the charity school. And the way she held herself, with her chin raised in that defiant way of hers, transformed this slender woman to a formidable one.

The crowd grew silent, watching as Miss Giles stared directly down her nose at Mr Latham.

"After all," she said casually, as if she didn't know she held the attention of the entire group, "a player is only as good as his ability to mask his emotions—is that not right?"

Her eyes roved around the table, looking for

confirmation from Mr Latham's peers, and they gave it, all nodding in turn.

"Bravo to Miss Derringer then, in so cleverly testing your wit, Mr Latham," said Miss Giles. "It is hardly her fault that you were found w-wanting."

The group around the table erupted into laughter. William found the amusement infectious, his generous mouth curving into a smile, eyes still on Miss Giles who now appeared small and inconsequential again having stepped back behind Charlotte.

The artfully delivered set-down made Mr Latham blush, and he threw down his cards, giving up his hand and cursing all women for their interfering ways. His friends cajoled him to lay aside his ill humour, and the young man found he could not keep pouting unless he wished to appear childish, and so he soon forced out a laugh, for the sake of his pride.

When the laughter had died down a little, and Charlotte had been applauded several times for her clever test, Miss Giles stepped forward and said something in her ear. William caught the word 'refreshment'. His sister nodded, a look of relief transforming her face, and both ladies moved off.

William started making his way towards them, intending to intercept their path, but was beaten to it by Mr Roberts.

"Might I escort you ladies to the drinks table?" the gentleman asked, bowing low over Miss Giles' hand that he had taken without permission.

William clenched his teeth. That dashed man Roberts was a perpetual flirt. He saw a look of hesitation on Miss Giles' face.

"Might I join you?" asked William, coming up beside

Mr Roberts. "Now I have finally found my sister, I wish to spend a little time with her on her first evening in Society."

"The more the merrier, I suppose," said Mr Roberts, his tone not matching the sentiment in the least.

Was that relief in Miss Giles' eyes?

CHAPTER 10

ry felt the tension fall away as she took Mr Derringer's arm. The less time she spent alone in Mr Roberts' company, the better.

Lady Amelia joined their party at the drinks table and was soon regaling the others with stories of the naughty mare her father had recently bought her.

"I think perhaps the young men who dare to insult my sister have much to fear from you, Miss Giles," Mr Derringer said in a voice that only Ary could hear.

Ary felt the tug at the corner of her mouth again. She had not seen Mr Derringer at the gaming table, but apparently he had seen her performance.

"I fear I was somewhat rude."

"I'm beginning to realise that you do not fear anything, Miss Giles."

How wrong he was.

"I could not have delivered a better set-down myself," he continued. "Nor a cleverer one, for you saved my sister from undue criticism while doing so. I hardly think he realised you had insulted him until it was all over. Where did you learn such skills?"

She could hardly tell him the truth. To do so would reveal more about her past than she was willing to share. It would mean telling him of her position at the charity school dealing with rambunctious young lads with no father figures to keep them in line. Boys she had frequently had to keep under control and interested in their school work. Not a thankless task, but an incredibly challenging one, and, if she was honest, not much different from dealing with that young pup Mr Latham.

But then Mr Derringer would ask how she went from charity school teacher to companion. Then he would ask how she became a charity school teacher, working his way backwards as people so often did when trying to piece together a picture. And then she would be forced to reveal her origins in the Foundling Hospital. Not a picture she was willing to reveal. No. She could hardly tell him the truth.

"I'm not sure I would call it a skill," she said at last.

"It seems I owe you my gratitude again."

"Hardly. Young men are just insensitive and foolish."

Was Mr Derringer... chuckling?

"How very astute of you. I trust my advancing years protect me from such censure?"

He was making her smile again. How did he manage to amuse her when she was trying her hardest to be cool towards him?

"Yes, Mr Derringer."

He bowed his head. "Thank you for defending her," he said earnestly, and then added with a gleam in his eye, "As a companion, you are so far not found w-wanting, Miss Giles."

The moment was interrupted by Mr Roberts, who called on Ary to give her opinion on chestnut mares. She could not tell him or the others that she could have no opinion for she had never learned to ride. Yet another part of her picture that she would keep obscured. So she gave an evasive answer and turned back to Mr Derringer, finding his eyes still on her. The keenness in his gaze was... unnerving.

⸙

MR ROBERTS INSISTED on escorting Ary through to supper. She agreed, not through any desire to do so, but rather because refusing would have seemed impolite.

"Have you been in Bath long?" he asked, after taking her on his arm.

"A week," she replied.

"So, you are not from these parts then—your role as Miss Derringer's companion has brought you here?"

"Yes." She would give him no more than she needed to.

"And how do you find it thus far?"

"Very well."

Unfortunately he seemed undeterred by her lack of enthusiasm.

"It is a pleasant enough city, but without the excitement of Town. I only sojourn here when London is devoid of Society. I find staying in the country, as some are wont to do, is a dreadful bore."

Ary thought of Duriel Hall and decided she would be quite content to be bored in the country if it meant living there. With that thought came the realisation that she was enjoying her new situation more than she had thought. Charlotte was a lovely girl and Mr Derringer was... pleasant. Was that the right word? No, Ary decided, it was not. But she did not wish to delve deeper into her unclear feelings towards Mr Derringer at this moment.

"Where did you live before coming to Bath—do not tell me, a country miss as Miss Sade surmised?"

Ary did not reply immediately, thinking on her response, but the delay was a mistake.

"Ah! I see Miss Sade was wrong in her calculations. Are you, in fact, from a city? You cannot be from north of here for you have no accent. You must be from Town."

By this time Mr Roberts had manoeuvred Ary to the far end of one of the supper tables, nowhere near Mr Derringer and his sister.

"Is that where your family reside?"

He held out a chair for her to sit down. She took it reluctantly.

"No."

"Where are they?"

To so direct a question she could offer nothing but the truth.

"I have no family, sir."

"No family," Mr Roberts echoed in false accents of melancholy. "But how sad for you, my poor angel."

Ary's pulse began to race. She had encountered men like Mr Roberts before. She remembered Mrs Stanaway's nephew, and the way that man had behaved when visiting the elderly woman. The way he had also taken a fancy to Ary and pitied her lack of family, until eventually he had cornered her after dinner one night and tried to seduce her. The drink had given him the courage to do so, but it had also made him clumsy, and Ary had managed to escape him and lock herself in her room. She had feigned illness after that night until the day his visit ended.

She felt the same suffocating feeling now with Mr Roberts breathing down her neck. She needed to get away from him. A servant placed a bowl of pale soup before her. While she had been hungry a short time before, she now felt sick thanks to Mr Roberts' interrogation.

"I think I should go back to Miss Derringer," said Ary, in a light voice, ignoring Mr Roberts' licentious gaze. "She will be needing me."

"And what of me—am I to be deprived of your company?" His lips curled into what was supposed to be a charming smile, but which appeared far more predatory in nature. "You have not even touched your soup."

Sat so close to him, she could see the traces of powder on his cheeks and the veins bulging in his neck.

"I know, but I find I am not hungry, and I'm afraid my duty is to my mistress."

Mr Roberts looked as though he was considering arguing.

"Very well," he sighed, like a cat who had tired of trapping the mouse and was about to let go of its tail. Ary could smell the wine on his breath. "Your devotion to your mistress only increases your delightfulness. I shall escort you to the Derringers, my angel."

Ary stopped herself from saying she did not need his escort. She did not wish to raise this man's ire. She had known men in their cups before and they were… unpredictable.

"Thank you, Mr Roberts."

He stood, offering her his arm, and she took it lightly. They made their way down the length of the table to where Mr Derringer and Charlotte sat with Lady Amelia and Miss Sade.

"Mr Roberts, we wondered what had become of you," said Mr Derringer.

Ary noted the edge to his voice and the hardness in the gaze he let fall on the gentleman standing beside her.

"Lost in the crowds," said Mr Roberts by way of explanation, "Lady Mires will be pleased to have her soiree so well attended."

Ary retracted her hand from his arm and slipped silently into an empty seat beside Charlotte. She did not touch the second bowl of soup that was placed before her, dipping her spoon into it several times before discarding it altogether. She allowed the conversation between Charlotte, Lady Amelia and Miss Sade to wash over her, all the while trying to put the intrusive gaze of Mr Roberts from her mind.

When she finally looked up from her soup, she saw Mr Roberts' interest had moved on, and he was busy flirting with Miss Sade who lapped up the attention like a starved kitten. Charlotte was relaxed and laughing, barely a trace of her stammer present. And then her eyes met Mr Derringer's.

He was looking directly at her, his green eyes so intense that she couldn't hold his gaze. What was in that look of his? Was it judgement he was directing at Ary? Did he think she had encouraged Mr Roberts' attentions?

The thought made her bridle. She drew her shoulders back and directed a level gaze back at him. She would not be made to feel inferior by another's poor behaviour.

But when she looked at Mr Derringer again, she realised that his hard gaze was no longer on her. No. In fact, it was focused entirely on Mr Roberts and the look in Mr Derringer's eyes had altered considerably. There was no longer a speculative look in their green depths. No, there was only one expression in them. Dislike. And Ary found herself strangely encouraged by the look.

CHAPTER 11

Despite the lateness of the night before, Ary woke early the next day. She had slept poorly, dreaming of overly friendly gentlemen with lecherous eyes, and at seven o'clock she gave up on sleep and rose.

She rang the bell for hot water and washed in the basin in her room. Slipping into her old dress, freshly laundered and free from the blood stain, she sat at her dressing table.

Ary ran a hand over her hair, unruly from sleep, and smiled ruefully. She should have braided it, but she hated to sleep with her hair bound and always paid the price the following morning. Taking up the ivory handled brush on her dressing table, she began dividing the brown locks and running the brush through it. The feeling was rhythmic and soothing.

It drew her back to her childhood in the Foundling Hospital where the girls would take it in turns to brush each other's hair with the one brush they had.

A sad smile formed on her face. She wondered where those girls were now. Likely not in the situation she was

—living as a companion to a respectable family with enough time to sit and leisurely brush her hair. Likely not.

She had detangled most of the hair now and was swishing the brush down its glossy brown lengths over and over. Not for the first time, Ary wondered whether her hair came from her mother or father. She always imagined her mother with darker hair, straighter than her own and a smile that warmed anyone it was bestowed on. Then she thought of her father. Had he abandoned her mother? Was that why Ary had been given up? Or had he died?

It had been some time since she had thought like this. She rarely allowed the locks on her past to be undone. It meant thinking of what could have been and that never boded well when there was enough in the present to occupy her. Her fingers sought out the wooden heart on her wrist instinctively. She pressed the thumb to the initials carved there, some comfort in the old familiar grooves and lines.

Outside the weather was turning. The wind had chased away the blue sky of the previous few days and brought with it white clouds and rain, spattering the window in fitful bursts.

A quiet knock sounded at the door, drawing Ary from her reverie.

"Yes?" She turned in her chair, allowing her hair to fall over her shoulders.

"G-good morning," said Charlotte shyly, hovering on the threshold after opening the door.

"Good morning, Miss Derringer." Ary rose and curtseyed, the thick curtain of her hair falling around her face. "Please come in."

"Oh, don't do that," said Charlotte, the stammer disappearing now she had been welcomed. "We're friends, aren't we?" Her cheeks rounded as she grinned and came to sit on Ary's bed. "And I told you to call me Charlotte. Or Lottie. William calls me Lottie."

Ary felt a prickling sensation across her skin at the mention of Mr Derringer.

"Are you waiting for my maid?" Charlotte asked.

Ary turned back and looked in the mirror, her hair fluffy and wild from being brushed. No, she hadn't been waiting for the maid. She had never had any help to dress her hair before coming here, always making do with simple styles she could manage herself.

Though Ary was thankful Charlotte had insisted on her maid dressing Ary's hair for the Mires' rout last night. When they had arrived at the party, Ary had immediately noticed all the high, curled and fantastical ways in which women wore their hair, with fruit and objects adorning them, and had known Charlotte had done her a huge favour.

"I had just thought of braiding it today."

"We're to go to Mrs Sade's to pay a call this morning. That's actually why I'm here. But, if you will allow me?" Charlotte gestured to Ary's hair.

"Oh, you needn't bother," Ary said, holding up her hands to halt Charlotte's advance towards her.

"Nonsense, I always wanted a sister whose hair I could dress. Unless"—she hesitated—"y-you would r-rather I d-didn't."

Charlotte's worried look tugged at Ary's heart and, though she was fairly certain their roles should be reversed in this moment, she gave a reassuring smile and nodded.

"Please do."

She turned back to the mirror on her dressing table and clasped her hands in her lap. She caught Charlotte smiling happily as she approached and picked up the brush.

"You have beautiful hair," Charlotte said as she ran the brush down its length.

"Not the rich colour of yours."

"I inherited it from my father. William's is the same."

Ary remembered Mr Derringer's hair from last night, lightly powdered, and thought it became him far better when he wore it *au naturel*.

"P-pass me the cushion?" Charlotte asked shyly.

Ary leant forward and picked up the small object from the dressing table, handing it to her would-be maid. Charlotte took it gingerly and placed it just above Ary's crown. She fetched some pins from an enamel pot on the table and began to fasten it in place.

"There should still be enough pomade in your hair from last night to hold it." Charlotte picked up a comb and began sectioning Ary's hair, slowly pulling pieces up and pinning them down the hole in the middle of the cushion. It didn't take long for the high style to begin to take shape and Ary saw in her reflection that it showed off the delicate point of her fine chin to advantage.

"Did you get your hair from your mother, or your father?" asked Charlotte, eyes on her work.

The question cut Ary to the quick, so in line with her previous thoughts it felt uncanny. "I don't know," she murmured in a moment of weakness. "They died when I was young."

"Oh." Charlotte paused in her ministrations,

dropping the latest lock of hair. "I-I'm sorry." Her hands grew less steady.

"Did your mother teach you to do your hair?" Ary asked, wanting to sooth the frayed nerves she knew she had caused.

A curve appeared at the side of Charlotte's mouth. "Yes."

Ary wondered if her mother would have taught her how to dress her hair if she had lived. Would they have sat like this, in some small house somewhere, while her father was out at work? She sighed, knowing the truth was likely far less idyllic. A woman did not give up her child when she had a modest house and a husband in employment.

"There." Charlotte put the last pin in place and looked at Ary in the mirror. "Will it d-do?"

Ary stared back at herself. The style was simple but elegant and suited her face very well.

"It's perfect," she reassured Charlotte, pushing the thoughts of her past back down where they were usually hidden and turning the key in the lock. "You do a far better job than I."

Charlotte grinned bashfully. "Shall I meet you downstairs for breakfast?"

Ary had been hoping to avoid the breakfast room. Mr Derringer would likely be there, and she did not wish to come under his curious gaze again. Especially not now, when she could feel her emotions running high. But she needed to eat, and she wished to please Charlotte after she had shown her such kindness in dressing her hair.

"Yes, I'll be down shortly."

Charlotte nodded, still smiling, and left. Ary turned back to stare at her reflection again—to wonder once again whose nose she had, whose eyes, whose mouth. Who had given her the thick brown hair she owned, or the challenging upturn of her chin? She would never know. She was alone in this world, without kin.

Downstairs a family breakfasted. A family of which she was not a part, in a home that was not her own—because she did not belong anywhere. God had not given her a home apart from him and she had made her peace with that long ago. She would continue to be the foundling, Miss Araminta Giles, traversing the world in her solitary state.

Rising from her dressing table her gaze fell from her face and she turned to leave her room and her reverie behind. It was time to earn her keep.

CHAPTER 12

$\mathcal{A}$ry need not have worried about seeing Mr Derringer at breakfast. He had eaten early and was busy on estate business. He did, however, join them for their morning call.

"Good morning, Miss Giles," he said when Ary and Charlotte came out to the waiting carriage.

"Oh no, William. You cannot go like that," said Charlotte in scandalised accents.

Mr Derringer looked down and Ary saw him take in his mud splattered boots and breeches.

"I believe, for once, my little sister is speaking sense." He glanced up, a mischievous look in his eyes.

"You are ghastly, and you'll make us late!" Charlotte cried.

"Have no fear, Lottie. I don't take as much time as you to get ready and shall be with you in less than ten minutes."

Ary saw another cheeky grin pass from brother to sister, and felt a prick of pain at the sight. They were so at ease in each other's company. There was a bond there that only family could give. Something she had never known.

Mr Derringer turned on his heel and strode back into the Hall.

"Let's get in the carriage to wait. The groom said there are hot bricks for both of us, and though the rain is holding, the day is chilling me right through," said Charlotte, no trace of her stammer.

Mr Derringer was back within the promised time, wearing a green wool suit that matched his eyes, clocked stockings and black leather shoes with plain silver buckles. Ary tried to ignore the tight fit of his jacket across his broad shoulders, and the smell of horse and mud that still lingered around him as he moved past her to sit opposite in the carriage. He banged the window behind his head and the vehicle started out on its rumbling journey.

"I trust you are not too tired after last night's gathering?" he asked, his eyes resting on Ary.

"No," she replied, holding his gaze for only a moment before directing her eyes out the window.

"And Lottie, you survived your first societal event!" He pumped a fist in the air and grinned. "You were a great success, sister, and I believe you were also well-received, Miss Giles."

"Yes. Mr R-Roberts didn't want to leave you alone." Charlotte started giggling.

It was easy for Charlotte to think it amusing that Mr Roberts had taken a fancy to her companion. Ary had hoped it wasn't so obvious, but apparently his attentions had not gone unnoticed. A man like Mr Roberts flirting with a *lady* was harmless. He would mean nothing by it, only playing the wit Society expected of him. But to flirt with Ary, a mere companion without any familial protectors—that was dangerous. It was exactly why she had handled him so carefully and eventually demanded to be taken back to the Derringers.

"He is a man who—" She hesitated, unsure how to put it without sounding uncivil. Her eyes met Mr Derringer's during her pause. "—likes his own conversation."

Charlotte giggled again and Ary was relieved to see Mr Derringer's eyes dancing.

"You did not find him too much of a distraction from chaperoning my sister?"

"William, that is ungenerous. Didn't you hear Miss Giles insisted on coming to sit with me after Mr Roberts took her away to supper? He complained she would rather spend time with me than him."

"Did you, Miss Giles?" There was a keenness in Mr Derringer's eyes.

"Yes."

"He is a f-frightful talker," said Charlotte, half-whispering the rude comment behind her hands.

"I'm afraid I agree with you, Lottie," said Mr Derringer, "though a gentleman should never speak ill of another."

Ary would not call Mr Roberts a gentleman. As she thought it, Mr Derringer caught her eye again and the knowing look in his made her feel as though he could read her thoughts. She felt the tips of her ears warm.

"First Mr Latham and now Mr Roberts—no man stands a chance against your wit, Miss Giles," said Mr Derringer, his green eyes dancing again.

"She is clever isn't she?" Charlotte agreed.

Ary, unused to such praise or attention, felt her ears

grow even warmer and sought refuge in looking down at her clasped hands. She could not be sure, but had that been approval from Mr Derringer? She had even seen a curve at the corner of his mouth. Why did the approval of this gentleman and his sister matter to her? They were only her employers, and this was only a temporary situation. Yet, as the carriage continued into Bath and the siblings began to talk about Lady Amelia's new horse, Ary couldn't help but feel... was it... content?

MRS SADE HAD BEEN PRATTLING on about the latest wallpapers from France, and the popularity of Chinese patterns, for the past ten minutes. In that time Mr Derringer had stolen several glances at Miss Giles. She sat demurely beside Charlotte on a scroll arm sofa.

He had seen Miss Giles discreetly tap Charlotte's arm when it was her turn to take a tea cup, and she had twice carried the conversation forward when Charlotte had got caught on a stammer. She neither dominated the company, nor did she fade entirely from view. She was quiet and dignified. He found it fascinating that one day she could be so forthright and commanding when it came to Mr Latham, and the next she could play the retiring companion whose only aim was to elevate her charge.

William had been more than a little relieved to hear that Miss Giles had discouraged Mr Roberts' flirtations. More than that, he felt pleased. Why would he be pleased? He frowned, knowing full well he should be listening to Mrs Sade, but having no desire to do so. It was only that he was pleased Miss Giles was turning out to be a woman of good character. Yes, that was all. He almost had the reassurance he needed to carry out his mother's wishes.

He thought back to the previous night and remembered seeing Miss Giles speaking to Mr Roberts when he had moved her to the other side of the supper room. William recognised now that Miss Giles' chin had been raised when she had spoken to Mr Roberts just before they had rejoined the group. That challenging chin of hers...

"What are you smiling at, Mr Derringer?" asked Miss Sade, cutting across her mother's conversation to speak to him.

"Nothing," he said too quickly. "Please don't let me interrupt your talk of the latest fashions. I'm sure Charlotte will be taking it all in so she may ask for her room to be re-papered the moment we leave."

"Oh, you must!" cried Miss Sade, as if they were speaking about taking medicine for a serious ailment or planning a military operation. "But tell me the truth, Mr Derringer," she continued, turning back to him, her eyes sparkling with interest. "What was it making you smile just now? I am sure it was not our talk of papers."

The woman did not want to give up. Worse, he saw her eyes darting between himself and Miss Giles. Had he been so indiscreet as to stare at her? *Again.*

"I must confess, I was just thinking of the Mires' rout last night. I beg your forgiveness, Mrs Sade. A joke that Lord Mires told me came to mind."

"Not at all," said the middle-aged woman generously. "My late husband was never interested in papers either."

"But I suspect he thanked you for decorating his home so beautifully?"

Mrs Sade smiled at the compliment and William hoped her daughter would now drop the line of conversation.

"We should very much like to see Duriel Hall again soon. My daughter does so love the gardens," said Mrs Sade transparently.

"They are beautiful at this time of year," William replied politely.

"We've been enjoying them h-haven't we, Ary?" Charlotte said, joining in and smiling.

"Oh yes?" Mrs Sade said, an eyebrow arching as she looked back over at Miss Giles. "Tell me Miss Giles, have we met before? I can't shake the feeling I recognise you."

William's jaw clenched involuntarily, and his fingers tightened on the chair arms.

"I do not think so, Mrs Sade." Miss Giles' words were polite, but cool, as she calmly returned Mrs Sade's inquisitive gaze.

Suddenly, the small and fine-figured Miss Giles appeared like a combatant, ready to defend herself. He could not blame her. Women like Miss Sade and her mother believed themselves subtle. Everyone else was under no such illusion. Miss Giles had already shown herself to be a woman of wit and William had no doubt that she was more than aware of the Sade's manoeuvring.

"Are you sure? It is unlike Mama to be wrong, Miss Giles. Perhaps you have relatives we might have the pleasure of being acquainted with."

William saw the white of Miss Giles' knuckles as she gripped her tea cup harder. There was a slight movement between his sister and her companion. Charlotte had dropped her hand to press Miss Giles' forearm. He frowned.

"I doubt it, Miss Sade. I am an orphan."

"Oh!" Miss Sade lifted a hand and pressed it against her breast.

"An orphan, you say?" asked Mrs Sade, apparently ignorant of the pain of the subject. "I wouldn't have known your parents in life?"

"I think perhaps this subject is not pleasant for Miss Giles," William cut in before she felt obliged to respond.

"It does so vex me, though," Mrs Sade complained. "For there is something most recognisable about you, Miss Giles."

"I am no lady, Mrs Sade, so I doubt you would have known my parents."

The blunt statement was uttered without the least shame.

"I see." Mrs Sade sniffed, the skin at either side of her nose pinching. "You consider yourself blessed, no doubt, to be companion to such a highly regarded family then."

William wondered what Miss Giles' response would be to such a condescending statement.

"I certainly do." Miss Giles gave Charlotte a kind smile.

"You are very good to have engaged her, Mr Derringer," Mrs Sade said, turning in her chair towards him and speaking about Miss Giles as if she were no longer present. "It is not everyone who would take a companion with such a lack of family."

Mrs Sade turned back to Miss Giles and said in the voice with which she would address a child, "Most mamas choose companions from their own families or at least from among their wider relatives."

William felt his heart compress at the sight of Miss Giles being addressed in such a manner. He shifted uncomfortably, uncrossing his legs and leaning forward to say something.

Charlotte suddenly spoke, her tone bright and her smile full of forced cheer.

"Has M-Miss Giles told you her C-Christian name?"

His sister could see as well as he how distasteful this line of conversation was.

"It is most unusual and very pretty—Araminta," said Charlotte.

"That is an unusual name," said Miss Sade, her fair brows arching in false interest.

"Araminta," Mrs Sade murmured thoughtfully, her gaze falling again on Miss Giles.

William was disturbed to see a dawning recognition on their hostess' face.

Before the dangerous conversation could continue, the front door sounded and whatever epiphany Mrs Sade was on the edge of, was mercifully cut short. William kept his eyes on their hostess, but it appeared the brief respite had made her doubt herself and she remained silent, tapping an index finger against her chin.

He resolved to say something to throw her completely off the scent when a footman came in to announce new callers and signal it was time for the Derringers and Miss Giles to leave. The tension William felt on leaving the Sade's house caused knots to form in his stomach. Mrs Sade had been close to realising who Miss Giles was. Worse, William was fast coming to the conclusion it would only be a matter of time before the truth came out.

CHAPTER 13

"What's that?" Charlotte asked Ary as they walked together in Sydney Gardens the following week.

The morning had dawned clear and bright. Any vestiges of rain had disappeared, and Charlotte had asked to drive into Bath for a walk in the gardens while the weather held.

Ary barely registered Charlotte's words. A moment ago Miss Derringer had been speaking of Miss Sade and it had thrown Ary's memories back to their morning call last week. She was not used to being scrutinised and the feeling had been most unpleasant. Ary was sure Miss Sade and her mother had meant it to be.

It was obvious to anyone with eyes that the young woman had set her cap at Mr Derringer—no matter how unaffected the gentleman appeared to be. For some reason, Miss Sade viewed Ary as a rival—a fact Ary would have found laughable if it had not led to such a calculated attack.

Ary was sure that was why Mrs Sade had persisted in

her assertion that she recognised her. No doubt they had mutual acquaintances with the deceased Mrs Stanaway and had found out Ary's lack of connections. Pointing that out in front of her employer had done an excellent job of highlighting Miss Sade's eligibility in comparison.

With an effort Ary drew her thoughts back to the present. "I'm sorry, Miss Derringer. What was it you wanted to know?"

"Charlotte—I told you. Lottie is even better," said Charlotte, squeezing Ary's arm where she held it. "That on your wrist—what is it?" She pointed with her free hand to the little wooden heart dangling from its ribbon.

Ary's heart sank. Now Charlotte was asking her questions too. Ary's instinctual reaction was to cut off any probing from her charge and offer no kind of answer. But when she looked at Charlotte, and saw the genuine interest in the young girl's eyes, she couldn't bring herself to do so.

"It was from my parents," Ary said quietly, eyes turning back to the path.

"Oh," Charlotte said in a reverent whisper. "Did they give it to you before th-they passed away?"

"Yes." Ary pressed her thumb against the indented initials. "I was told my father carved it."

"That's very lovely."

Their walk had slowed as they spoke.

"May I ask—how did they die?"

Even after all these years the question still carried with it a sting. Normally Ary could shrug it off, just as she had done many times before when a nosy individual wanted to know why a comely young woman, with the bearing of a lady, was teaching at a charity school, or companion to an elderly widow. But Charlotte's questions were not those of a busybody. They were born from genuine care and interest.

"You do not have to a-answer, i-if you d-don't want to," Charlotte said. "I sh-shouldn't have a-asked."

"It's all right," Ary said quickly. "According to my mother's letter to me, my father died at war. I'm not sure about my mother. She left me at the Foundling Hospital as a baby. They told me she died shortly after, but I never found out how, or where she or my father are buried."

That was the truth, the shameful truth. She had been delivered to the Foundling Hospital with a letter from a mother she had never known and the wooden heart that dangled from her wrist.

Her mother had written that Ary was loved by both her parents, but her father had died, and she was very ill and could no longer keep her daughter. She had told Ary never to let go of the heart—a token symbolising her parents' love. If she recovered, her mother promised to come back for Ary, knowing her by the heart. But her mother had never come back and Ary had never discovered the truth.

Had her father really died, or had he abandoned her mother? Had her mother really been ill and not recovered, or had she abandoned Ary too?

"Were you very young?"

"A baby."

"That's so awful—never to have known your mother."

Pity, Ary had learned long ago, could undo her. She had no security in which to stop and bemoan her difficulties. If she did not carry on with life, there was no one else who would do so on her behalf.

"I cannot imagine what that would be like." Charlotte's words broke into her melancholy reverie.

"It was not all bad," said Ary, steering the conversation away from the sadness of her childhood. "I was fortunate enough to gain a benefactor when I was still a girl. Those in charge at the Foundling Hospital said it was because I showed promise. My sponsor funded my education and that was how I could gain a position as a schoolmistress."

There were plenty worse off than Ary. She had been fortunate indeed to gain such a benefactor. None of the other children had been blessed with one. Without the extra education her benefactor had allowed, she would have been apprenticed as a servant. Instead her studies had secured her position as schoolmistress and then as companion to Mrs Stanaway and now with the Derringers.

"And that has brought you to me," said Charlotte, smiling sweetly at her. "For that I am thankful, especially because of how quick-witted you were with Mr Latham." Her eyes gleamed mischievously. "I think William was very impressed."

The mention of Mr Derringer caused a shiver to run through Ary. There was still something about her employer's interest in her which, though not over friendly like Mr Roberts, she did not find completely comfortable. In truth, she was relieved when he had said he would not join them for a walk today.

"He isn't often, you know," Charlotte continued. "He has been so serious since Mama and Papa died. But he has seemed more light-hearted lately."

Ary was about to reply when they were hailed from behind.

"Good morning!"

Both ladies turned to see Mr Roberts approaching. A rush of disdain flooded Ary. She kept Charlotte's arm firmly within her own as they curtseyed together.

"What a fine day it is, and finer still now I have happened upon you two lovely ladies. Your brother does not attend you, Miss Derringer?"

"No, Mr Roberts. He is with his steward this morning."

"Ah, no rest for the wicked—or the abominably good in the case of your brother." Mr Roberts winked at both women. "Might I offer my company then, in lieu of your brother?"

There was no way to politely decline this offer.

"Of c-course, Mr Roberts. Though we will not be as m-much amusement as my brother, I'm s-sure," Charlotte answered.

It was prettily said, and though she stammered, Ary was pleased to see that her charge was showing more confidence in conversation. That said, she would have preferred to watch such confidence being displayed towards anyone but Mr Roberts.

"Nonsense," said the gentleman, taking Charlotte onto his arm, breaking the two women apart, and coming to Ary's side to do the same.

Everything in her resisted taking it, but again, politeness bade her take it even though he might consider it a misplaced sign of her favour. She took his arm and all three set off together.

"May I say, you are both looking radiant today?"

Charlotte let out a nervous giggle.

"You will be the belle of your Season, I have no

doubt, Miss Derringer," said Mr Roberts, flattery coming to him as easily as barking did to a terrier.

"Y-you are very kind, Mr Roberts," said Charlotte, blushing becomingly.

"And you, Miss Giles. Can I look forward to receiving pretty words from you?"

"How can I, sir," Ary ground out, "when you are using them all up for our benefit?"

She had meant the words as a set-down, but Mr Roberts laughed.

"A fine wit, you are!"

At that moment a party came into view on the bridge ahead.

"Amelia!" Charlotte cried, seeing her friend in the group. "May I go and speak to her, Miss Giles?"

Ary spotted Lord and Lady Mires with their daughter and deemed it appropriate to allow Charlotte to stop and talk with her friend.

"Yes, Miss Derringer, we can head towards them now."

Perhaps if they met with the Mires' party, she might be able to dilute some of Mr Roberts' intolerable flirting among the interactions of far less oily individuals.

Unfortunately, Charlotte's naivety got the better of her. Ary watched with discomfort as her charge skipped ahead to greet her friend, leaving Ary with the gentleman in question.

"Young girls—always so delightful in their exuberance."

Ary murmured her agreement, trying to pick up her pace so she might meet with the Mires family sooner and not have to converse alone with this man. She pulled gently against Mr Roberts' arm, but if he noticed he did not admit it, for he kept a slow meandering pace.

"Now I may enjoy your company to myself, Miss Giles." His voice was lower now and that disconcerting smile of his was back as he looked down at her. "What a blessing it is to me that the Derringers should employ such a beautiful companion."

He clamped his arm to his side, preventing her from pulling her own away. The action pulled her even closer to him. Too close for propriety. She could feel the warmth of him through his jacket. A sick feeling curled itself around her stomach.

"Tell me, Miss Giles, do you find me handsome?"

His words were far outside the bounds of propriety now. There was no way Ary would be spoken to like this if she were a lady. But Mr Roberts knew she was not. He knew she was alone in the world and an easy target for his ungentlemanly attentions.

Despite her best efforts to keep her emotions calm, Ary began to panic. Her dark eyes widened as she glanced over to where Charlotte was now busy chatting away to Amelia and her parents. None of them had noticed Ary hadn't joined them yet. The longer she was with Mr Roberts alone like this, the more likely they were to cause talk.

"Your charge is safe," said Mr Roberts, following her gaze. "We can enjoy a little *private* walk."

Without warning, Mr Roberts dragged her to the left, away from the bridge and down a side path.

"Mr Roberts, no," Ary spat out as he pulled her with far more force than she was expecting, causing her to stumble. "I must return to Miss Derringer. Please take me back."

Her desperate tone was lost on the man.

"Come now, your maidenly concern is well-played, but do not tell me that you are not enjoying it being just the two of us? I shall not believe it."

They were almost out of sight of the party now. If Ary was found like this, compromised in such a fashion, she would lose her position.

"Mr Roberts," Ary said, voice firmer. "I must return to my party now." She pulled her arm again, but again failed to break free.

"What? Before we have our little tête-à-tête? You do not have to be shy with me, my girl. *I* have no wish to be shy with you."

He swung around to face her, snaking his free arm around her waist.

"You haven't answered my question yet." He looked down at her, and from this angle his attractive face appeared overbearing and grotesque. "Don't you think me handsome?"

The net was closing in. Ary's breathing quickened.

"If you were to think me handsome, I might keep you company. There is no sense in a beautiful creature like you being alone in the world. I can provide you with companionship and... protection from others."

The sick feeling heightened. He was leveraging her vulnerability. He pressed closer to her. She had to do something now.

Snatching her hand away from Mr Roberts with far more force than she had used before, she managed to break free. Before he could react, she brought the heel of her boot down on his toe. He let out a cry of anguish, then she brought her knee up between his legs and he doubled over making a wheezing sound.

She didn't wait another moment, spinning on her heel and charging straight back the way they had come. Before she'd made it three steps, she collided with another person. It sent her careering backwards until two hands clamped onto her upper arms to steady her. Not recognising the action as friendly, she wrenched away, eyes wide, and brought back her gloved hand ready to strike.

"Woah!" came the cry.

The newcomer grabbed her wrist to halt her hand before it struck. When her gaze eventually fell on their face, she realised with a start that it was Mr Derringer.

Her breath caught. She gulped for air, pulling back her hand from its restraint. Her employer released her immediately and she waited, standing between the two gentlemen, breathing rapidly.

Mr Derringer's expression was hard, eyes flicking between Ary and the injured Mr Roberts behind her. What was he thinking? A muscle at the corner of his jaw flexed as he ground his teeth.

"Miss Giles," Mr Derringer said at length, enunciating her name carefully.

She could still hear Mr Roberts wheezing behind her.

"My sister sent me in search of you when I came upon her with Lord and Lady Mires."

She forced herself to look Mr Derringer in the eye, even though all she wanted to do was disappear at this moment. She could not stop shaking. Would she be sacked on the spot? She would have no references. Nowhere to go. What would he tell Charlotte?

She clasped her hands before her, attempting to still the shaking, and raised her chin. She could hear scuffling behind her and assumed Mr Roberts was making a hasty attempt at hiding his pain.

"Will you allow me to escort you back"—Mr Derringer held out his arm—"before you are found to be missing?"

Ary looked at him, then risked a glance back at Mr Roberts who was still clutching his breeches and looking very red in the face. She could not stay here with Mr Roberts, but nor did she feel she had the courage to go with her employer. Mr Derringer looked so… angry.

"Please wait for me over there." Mr Derringer pointed to the path behind him.

Ary exhaled slowly, willing her breath to come out smoothly. Nodding once, she followed his instructions and went to wait a short distance away. She could see Mr Derringer lean in to Mr Roberts. He was murmuring something to him. The gentleman, whose colour was still dreadfully heightened, flashed angry eyes at the interloper. Mr Derringer finished what he was saying with a nod of finality and turned on his heel, leaving Mr Roberts there.

As Mr Derringer approached, Ary drew in another gusty breath and with it all the courage she could muster before taking his offered arm. She might fear what punishment Mr Derringer would deal out, but she felt safer on his arm than staying with the lascivious Mr Roberts.

CHAPTER 14

"Miss Giles," William began, halting their walk so he could face her.

They had returned to one of the main paths. His sister and the Mires party had moved off to greet more acquaintances, affording himself and Miss Giles some time alone.

"It was not my intention to go with Mr Roberts down that path," Miss Giles blurted out. "I would never do so willingly."

In spite of his best attempts to look her in the eye, she would not meet his gaze. If she had, perhaps she might have seen in his expression that she had no need to defend herself. He did not blame her for what had just transpired. The situation had been as plain as day when he had come upon them.

Miss Giles still looked dreadfully pale, and she may be lifting her chin and drawing her shoulders back in a stance of courage, but the slight tremor in her voice gave away her true feelings. That man Roberts deserved a thrashing.

"I did not think for a moment that it was your intention to go with Mr Roberts," he said with feeling.

Her mouth parted, her eyes widening, but she didn't say anything.

"Are you hurt?"

Her sleeves and bodice were misaligned from where Mr Roberts had been grabbing at her. Apart from that she appeared unscathed. His gaze moved back from her body to her face, and he noted the wary look in her eyes.

"You have nothing to fear from me." He hid the angry tone from his voice, softening it.

Her shoulders relaxed a fraction.

"No," she said, colour appearing back in her cheeks.

"No?"

"No, I am not hurt."

William breathed more easily.

"Will you allow me to escort you back to my sister now or would you rather go straight home?"

"I would like to go to Miss Derringer," she replied, taking his arm again tentatively.

He set the pace slower than before. He wished to give Miss Giles time to recover before they rejoined the others. If he wasn't so concerned over her welfare he would have stopped to beat Roberts. He had never liked that man, even when they were at university together.

"He should not have behaved like that," William said quietly.

He looked over his shoulder. There was no sign of Mr Roberts. Hopefully he had returned home to nurse his wounded pride.

"I am only a companion," Miss Giles replied. "Gentlemen are wont to try their hand."

William felt his stomach twist at the resignation in Miss Giles' voice. Resignation born from years of mistreatment. Loathing for her tone washed over William. Loathing for himself. Knowing that his family could have—should have—done something years ago.

"You've suffered this before?"

She took a moment to answer. When she did, some of the hardness was gone from her voice. "When you have no parents to protect you, you must learn from a young age how to protect yourself."

To William's surprise he heard her laugh. But all joy was drained from the sound.

"I must sound like some novel's heroine —melodramatic."

"You are not being dramatic," William said firmly. "What just happened is a serious thing. I will not allow it to happen again. Do you understand?" He looked down at her and she returned his gaze, her brown eyes unguarded for once.

She gave a single nod.

"You are under my... my family's protection," he corrected himself. "If you ever fear anything like that happening again, you are to tell me."

"Yes, Mr Derringer."

They had been speaking so freely he had almost forgotten their respective positions.

A few minutes later they caught up with his sister and the Mires family. The incident with Mr Roberts was not mentioned, and the trade Miss Giles had made of one escort for another was brushed over easily enough by Mr Derringer.

William half attended the conversations that

followed. He could not stop picturing Miss Giles struggling to get away from Mr Roberts. He wondered how many times she had faced such men.

Anger on her behalf and the protectiveness he had felt earlier came to the fore. He had been waiting and measuring Miss Giles' character. He had seen how she had cared for his sister. Now he had seen her spurn a gentleman's advances despite the fact he would likely have offered her some security for his attentions.

William didn't need to wait any longer. He knew the kind of woman Miss Giles was. He needed to tell her the truth. But so much time had passed, he realised he had no idea where to start.

ARY COULD NOT SLEEP.

The incident with Mr Roberts that morning had shaken her. She hated that another might hold such power over her. The power to take advantage. The power to make her feel like this. She did not give the power freely. She had learned long ago that she must maintain control. That she had to be strong. That no one else would be strong on her behalf. It was down to her alone.

But in this moment she did not feel strong. The humanness that resided behind her strong surface was seeping through the cracks Mr Roberts had made. She sought refuge in escape, and it was books that opened that door for her. Ever since Miss Drench had allowed her to borrow her own few books, Ary had found comfort between the covers of cloth or leather-bound pages.

It was not just her interest in the subjects that gave her relief, though her interests were broad. Books on history, geography, noble families, art—she had devoured them all. It was that those words, flowing into sentences, building themselves up into other worlds, gave her a place to step into. A relief from reality. Her thoughts and feelings were occupied with topics outside her own life. She would float between reality and this written world, resting in a place where the loneliness and worries could not touch her.

The only other place she felt that way was in church when the vicar prayed. When she was still and focused on her insignificance before a sovereign God.

But late at night, like now, when she couldn't sleep and prayer had been exhausted, she needed words on the page. She sat up in bed, her candle burned half-down, a shawl around her shoulders to ward off the night-time chill. Glancing at the side table again she sighed. The three books Mr Derringer had given her were read and finished.

Duriel Hall had been silent for the last half-hour. If she went down to the library now, surely that would be acceptable. If not acceptable, at least Mr Derringer had given her permission. True, he probably wouldn't think she would be taking up his offer to borrow more books in the middle of the night, but dire circumstances forced her hand.

Decision made, she swung her legs over the side of the bed and rose to redress. It did not take long—the action of dressing without a maid long-known and familiar. She drew the gown on over her arms, placing the stomacher on her front and pinning the gown closed down its sides. Her stockings were rolled on quickly enough and then she ran a hand over her recently braided hair, assuring herself that the twists of the plait were still intact. She finally re-wrapped the shawl around her shoulders before picking up the candle in its holder.

There was half a pillar left—enough to shed light on her midnight travels. She scooped up the three books on her bedside table, tucking them under her arm, and eased open the bedroom door.

A waft of cool air ran over her face when she looked out into the darkness. After a moment her eyes adjusted, and she realised it was not completely without light. There were a few lone candles still burning low in the wall sconces. Downstairs she saw a faint light too. Someone in the house was still up. She hesitated on the threshold. What if it was Mr Derringer? Memories of his actions and words in Sydney Gardens came to mind.

'If you ever fear anything like that happening again, you are to tell me.'

He had offered her protection. Not like Mrs Stanaway's nephew or Mr Roberts, who demanded something in return. A shiver ran through her. Was that an unpleasant feeling? No, it was... relief. She wasn't afraid of Mr Derringer. Even if it was him still up in the house, he would likely be in his study. The library would be empty. It would be waiting for her.

The thought of retreating into her empty room and the dark thoughts that waited for her there drove her forwards. She stepped from the room, drawing her door to a close behind her and began down the hall. Her stockinged feet were silent as she padded along, though the payment for her quietness was freezing toes.

The large square spiral of the Hall's staircase appeared even larger and more forbidding in the half-light of the few candles still burning. Ary hurried down them, telling herself there was nothing to be scared of in the shadows, and reached the cold marble floor of the hall. She headed straight for the library door and was relieved when she opened it and found the room lit and a fire half-burned down in the grate.

She closed the door with a soft click and made her way over to the warmth of the fire. Placing the books on the mantle, she bent down to put another log on those already surrendered to the flames. Not the action of a lady, she thought, but one she would be thankful for while she chose a new book. Rising too fast, without paying attention to the candle still in her hand, hot wax fell onto her skin.

She cursed.

Placing the candle holder next to the books on the mantle, she wrung her hand, willing the stinging to stop. Glancing down she saw the wax was already dried, and flicked it off her knuckle before putting the joint to her lips.

"You are rather accident prone when it comes to your hands, aren't you?"

Ary jumped, spinning around, searching for the voice's owner. She was sure it was Mr Derringer, but she couldn't locate him.

"Here," he said gently, stepping out from a window alcove and raising the book in his hand in a kind of salute.

"I came to get a book," Ary said quickly, by way of explanation.

"And to bank the fire." He was smiling at her, and the way he did so sent a wave of warmth through her body.

"Yes."

"Don't let me stop you," Mr Derringer said, holding his arms wide to encompass the shelves of books surrounding them.

"Thank you." Ary turned back to the mantle and picked up the three books she had discarded there. "Where shall I put these?"

"Just leave them there," he said, gesturing with the book in his hand to a side table. "I'll put them away."

She did as she was bid, inadvertently disturbing Jupiter who had been laying half-asleep against one of the table legs. The dog rose, stretching with his haunches in the air and his head between his front paws, and then came to lick Ary's hand.

She smiled, bending down to scratch behind his ears, and then pushed him away. Since coming to the Hall she had grown used to the animal and found his presence reassuring now she was alone with Mr Derringer. It wasn't that he made her feel uncomfortable. No, that was not at all what she felt when she was with him.

Turning to the shelves, she scanned the rows of books. She must choose fast. Being alone with the master of the house wasn't strictly proper. Her eyes ran over the spines near her. Topography, heraldry, geology. None appealed. She moved to the next case and perused the titles. *Britannia Romana: Or, The Roman Antiquities of Britain,* she could read that. She reached for it.

"Can I ask you a question?" Mr Derringer's voice caused her to pause, the book half-descended.

She brought it down and held it against her chest, turning to meet his gaze.

"Yes."

"Are you struggling to sleep because of what happened this morning?"

Ary felt the question sharply. It cut through the facade she had thought shielded her from scrutiny. The mask which portrayed her as calm and unaffected by the horrors of life. Had she allowed it to slip?

"I... " she had been intending to lie. To say no. That she wouldn't let such a pathetic man's actions affect her. But the words died on her lips as she returned Mr Derringer's frank gaze.

She opted for diversion instead. "I wish to thank you for what you did for me in Sydney Gardens."

"I should not have had to do it."

Was this when she would receive her reprimand?

"Mr Roberts should have acted better."

She had not been expecting that.

"But you did," she said simply, the thought coming out in words before she could stop it.

She was unused to being indebted to another. To having someone look out for her care. While she might not relish the idea that she had relied on someone else to help her out of that awful situation, Ary had to admit there was some comfort in another coming to her aid. "I am thankful for it."

"You don't need to thank me—it's no more than a gentleman would do. *Should* do," he added.

"That may be," she said, bitterness tracing her words, "but I have known gentlemen to *not* act in such a way."

She saw his mouth open, but whatever he was about to say never came. Ary dared not wait any longer, aware of the impropriety of staying here with him, and feeling that something was passing between them in this moment that was dangerous. She needed to go back upstairs to safety with this book to occupy her mind.

"You didn't answer my question," he said, halting her escape as he stepped forward into her path. "You have nothing to fear here." As if to reiterate the point, he took half a step back from her. "This is your home now. You are safe here."

The words were oddly intimate. Not at all the things she would expect to hear from an employer. And yet they were things she had yearned to hear for many years. A part of her deep within wanted this—a place of refuge and safety.

But she was employed to be here. This relationship was conditional, and it might be taken from her at any time. Mr Derringer did not understand that like she did. He was promising things that he may end up reneging on in the future.

He reached towards where her hands were clasped around the book. She was about to move away but something stilled her. She allowed him to take the fingers of the hand she had burned.

She so rarely touched another. The feel of his fingers, larger than her own, and rougher. Sparks ran down her arm, but the sensation was not an unsettling one. No, this feeling was so entirely different from the disagreeableness of her encounter with Mr Roberts. She didn't feel unsafe with Mr Derringer.

"Do you need ointment for your hand?"

"No—it is nought."

He chuckled. The sound was deep and pleasing.

"So strong, Miss Giles. I had not expected that."

Ary's brow crinkled.

The look on her face seemed to make him remember

himself. The softness in his expression was replaced by a proper politeness and he cleared his throat, dropping her hand.

"Good night, Miss Giles."

She felt the loss of his touch, though she knew it was for the best.

"Good night, Mr Derringer."

William was up early the next day in spite of his late night. He had dreamt of Miss Giles. Her small figure had stood resolute in his subconscious mind. She had watched him with those deep dark eyes of hers. His dream-self had reached out and touched her hands and he had started speaking to her. He didn't know exactly what words he had used in the dream, but he knew the feeling behind them. He had been telling her the truth—and she had turned away from him and left.

The memory of the dream caused William to grimace. Though the dream itself grew less distinct over time, the feeling it evoked did not. A feeling of failure. He fingered the wooden heart in his hand, pressing his thumb to the initials just as he had seen Miss Giles do. He looked down at the object as he sat at his desk.

Mary Derringer, his mother's name. Anne Goodwin, his mother's best friend. He pulled a letter from his desk drawers and read it again as he had done many times since his mother's passing,

Dear Mary,

I know circumstances have pulled us apart, but you are still my dearest friend, and I trust this plea for help will not fall on deaf ears.

Luke has died in service at Warburg in Prussia. It seems a cruel twist of fate when we won that battle to have lost him there. It has been made more painful by accusations of dishonourable behaviour leading to his death at the hands of his own superiors. I will not believe such things of Luke. It is —was—so wholly against his character.

I am left alone in the world with no support after my family cut me off on my marriage, and it is worse—though how it can be I can barely make sense of—I am dying, my dearest Mary.

I have a baby daughter, Araminta, and when I die, she will have no one. I wrote to my own family, but they will not return my letters. I fear the scandal surrounding Luke's death has done me no favours.

But it is not little Ary's fault. She is an innocent babe. It is too cruel.

I was left with no other choice than to give her up to the Foundling Hospital. I cannot describe the pain of leaving her there, but the thought that she might suffer further by staying with her ill mother, is too much to bear. I had prayed, fervently prayed, that God might heal me of this affliction so that I might go and retrieve Ary, but he has not and now death seems close.

Please, I beg of you, if you ever had love for me, from one mother to another, care for my child. She is innocent of all this and yet will bear the greatest

suffering. I have left her with my wooden heart.
You remember those two hearts Luke made for us?
I trust you still have its twin. You shall know
Araminta by this. Please find her, and care
for her.
I am selfish, for I find as I grow weaker, that I
look forward to being with my Luke again. I
know your heart is good and loving. You were the
only friend who kept writing to me after I
married. I trust you will care for my child, and
with that thought I can finally rest, my dear
friend.
Love,
Anne

It was this letter, and the wooden heart, that William's mother had told him about on her deathbed. She had found Araminta all those years ago, but rather than take her in for fear of the family's reputation, she had become an anonymous benefactor for the girl's care and education.

It was her dying wish, that William find Araminta. She had made William swear it. So after they had laid their mother to rest, William had gone in search of the girl, and had found her serving as companion to Mrs Stanaway.

William had made a plan. He had decided the safest way to bring her into their lives was conditionally, as a companion to his sister. If she did not prove to be a lady of quality, he would not bring her into their lives permanently. He could simply settle an amount of money on her and leave her to live her own life. But now he knew Araminta, the woman she had grown to be, and he wasn't sure he had made the right decision in how to handle it.

Suddenly his plan seemed callous and unfeeling. He had kept the truth from this woman, who had no family, and no knowledge of who she was. He had planned a way to help her that involved no risk to his own family, and he knew in his heart that it was not what his mother had asked of him. William realised he had chosen the same path his mother had done, all those years ago. He had decided that money was the solution to the problem —the perfect way to assuage his guilt.

William wanted to tell Miss Giles the truth. He knew it was the right thing to do, and yet he did not know where to start. He did not want to admit he had been testing her. That her stay here had been conditional— that he had set standards for her to attain. It all seemed so heartless now, where it had appeared so practical before. The shame of his actions burned into his soul and fear grew within him as he considered the question which haunted his waking moments. What would Ary think of him when he told her?

WHEN ARY ENTERED Mr and Mrs Devenham's ballroom two weeks later, she had the distinct impression that people were staring.

At first she thought perhaps Charlotte was winning the attention, for she did look beautiful in pink silk this evening. But she soon noticed that the eyes did not linger on her charge, but on herself, and it wasn't with any kind of admiration. No, it was intrigue in their eyes.

Her skin prickled with the knowledge of being so keenly observed. Had the story of her incident with Mr Roberts become known? She cringed at the thought. Surely Mr Roberts had not been spreading it abroad? He would be hard put to paint himself in a generous light should he recount the tale. Mr Derringer then? Ary discounted that as soon as it came to mind. He had saved her, not to mention been solicitous of her feelings. No, of his integrity she could be sure.

Had someone seen the encounter then?

"Ah, Miss Derringer." Miss Sade came upon them. She was looking particularly alluring in a gown of dusky pink, her hair coiffured and powdered, and a delicate pearl necklace encircling her fine throat. Ary saw her look pointedly at Charlotte's gown which was in a similar shade. "How fortunate we are to have your company this evening."

"Good evening, M-Miss Sade." Charlotte stammered under her gaze. She curtseyed nervously.

"Your brother is not with you?" Miss Sade looked over their shoulders, hoping to see the object of her relentless affections.

"He is speaking with Mr Rufford, I b-believe."

"Ah well," said Miss Sade, and then with tones of resignation, "Miss Giles."

"Miss Sade."

"You are the talk of the evening already." Miss Sade's eyes gleamed.

"Oh?" Ary's tone was less than interested. She had no desire to play this woman's games.

"Why yes, because your secret is at last found out!"

"S-secret?" Charlotte questioned, looking between Miss Sade and Ary.

Ary resisted the urge to roll her eyes. The annoying woman was obviously playing some childish game.

Before Miss Sade could continue, Lady Amelia came bowling into the conversation. She pounced on Charlotte, stealing her away to attend the conversation with her brother, Mr Rufford, and now Mr Davy. The latter two gentlemen were discussing racing their curricles between Bath and Wells.

"It was your name that finally gave you away, Miss Giles."

Ary felt the hairs on the back of her neck rising. What did her name have to do with anything?

"That, and the fact my Mama recognised you."

How could her mother have possibly recognised Ary? They had never met before.

"Oh, you are surprised. That's to be expected. Your mother would have died when you were very young, but my Mama says you look quite like her."

Cold stole over Ary.

"Anne Goodwin, that is, though Giles was her married name. That's what threw Mama off, for not many knew what Miss Goodwin's married name was, it being such a disgraceful match."

Miss Sade's words sounded further and further away. Anne Goodwin. A.G. *A. G.*, Ary pressed the heart on her wrist. It couldn't be.

"Apparently your father died in dishonour in the war."

The more statements Miss Sade made, the sicker Ary felt. She could not tell if what she was hearing was true, but she had an awful feeling it could not all be lies.

"I suppose that's why Mr Derringer has engaged you. His late mother was great friends with Miss Goodwin—

before her fall from grace, of course. He no doubt took pity on you."

Every word was like a fresh arrow, burying itself into the softness of Ary's feelings, causing emotions to bleed out of her which she neither wanted to acknowledge nor feel. If there was any truth to what Miss Sade was saying, then the providence which had brought her to Duriel Hall, which she had thanked God for, was no providence at all. It was no twist of fate or work of God that had brought her here. It was Mr Derringer.

⟶ ❦ ⟵

ARY STRUGGLED TO FOCUS. She stood on the edge of the dancefloor watching Charlotte standing up with Mr Roberts, but rather than consider her charge's undesirable match, she found every one of her thoughts punctuated by Miss Sade's revelation.

The heinous woman had delivered a parting shot about Ary's being quite below the Derringers' station, particularly that of Mr Derringer, before going to dance the next set with a red-faced gentleman who laid claim to a barony.

Ary had made a swift recovery, bandaging some of the wounds the woman's words had left and managing to contain her emotions. In truth, the shock had caused a numbness to steal over her.

"She looks very well—though I could wish her another partner."

Mr Derringer had appeared beside her. He had two full glasses of punch and handed one to Ary.

"Thank you." She took it, and sipped the liquid without tasting it.

She hoped the drink would fortify her. Now was not the time to speak to Mr Derringer. She needed time to collect her scattered thoughts, but the less rational half of her was crying out to say something.

She looked down, her gloved hand tight on the glass, and wondered how hard she would have to press for it to shatter in her hands.

"Ah," Mr Derringer said, "I am being hailed by Lord Mires. Please excuse me." He bowed and left her again and Ary was thankful he had been with her only briefly.

There had been questions on the tip of her tongue, and angry accusations, that she would have regretted uttering. She looked back towards Charlotte as the final refrain from the music played out, and saw the couples bowing and curtseying before breaking away from their previous shapes and leaving the dancefloor.

Ary saw Mr Roberts approaching, with Charlotte on his arm, and tensed. She wasn't sure what reaction to expect from him after their altercation.

"Miss Giles," he said, a false smile on his face and his voice devoid of pleasure.

Ary gave him the merest incline of her head.

"Ary, how pleased I am to have found you." Charlotte pulled away from Mr Roberts with slightly too much joy, and looped her arm through Ary's.

"Mr Roberts, thank you for the dance."

"Your servant," Mr Roberts said, bowing theatrically. "I am flattered to have had such a beautiful partner."

This bold comment caused Charlotte to colour deeply.

"You are not dancing this evening, Miss Giles?" he

asked, turning back to Ary with a look of malicious challenge in his eyes.

He knew very well that if she had been asked, she would have been dancing too. So he would insult her subtly—that was to be his way of recovering his lost pride. So be it.

"Not yet, Mr Roberts." She wished to tell him she saw no suitable partners present, but decided it was best not to goad him.

"I suppose you were not taught to dance at the Foundling Hospital?"

The blunt words were delivered so casually that it took Ary a moment to comprehend them. She was still reeling when he spoke again.

"I do so admire you for taking her on as a companion, Miss Derringer. Not every young woman would want the daughter of a disgraced lady for their companion."

The words were not meant to be proper, or anywhere in the vicinity of politeness. Ary recognised before her a man all the more dangerous because his pride had been damaged by her refusal of his advances. But worse, she was understanding all those staring eyes. It was not just Miss Sade who carried the tale of Ary's parentage. The rumour was running throughout the ball, and soon Bath Society would be ringing with it.

"Mr Roberts, I am sure th-that is n-not proper," Charlotte stammered, shocked by his words but compassion preventing her silence.

"My apologies for speaking so freely." Mr Roberts bowed low again, but this time the action was as insincere as his words. "I understood it to be common knowledge that Miss Giles is the orphan daughter of a

Mrs Anne Giles, née Goodwin, and a common soldier who died in mutiny against his superiors. That is what Mrs Sade has told me. Half the attendees are speaking of it. Did your brother not tell you? No doubt he considered your ears too innocent, for they are. But I very much doubt yours are, Miss Giles, after growing up in such a manner. No one thought Miss Goodwin would sink so low as to abandon her child, but then her judgement was clearly—"

Mr Roberts was shocked into stopping by the contents of Ary's glass being dashed over his face. He blinked in disbelief, droplets of ratafia running down his skin and dripping off his nose.

"Ary!" Charlotte gasped.

"Who the devil do you think you are!" Mr Roberts shouted angrily, attracting the attention of the rest of the room.

Conversation died away and Ary felt the prickling sensation down her back again as a great multitude of eyes turned on her.

"Just the sort of common behaviour we should expect from you," Mr Roberts snapped, dabbing his face with a handkerchief.

A great deal of rouge and powder came off on the white linen and he was left with a patch of sallow coloured skin on show.

"I say! What's all this?" cried an elderly gentleman.

Ary watched the older man saunter over as if she were in a day dream. He wore an old-fashioned bob wig, an ancient silk suit, and a diamond winked from the handle of his ebony cane. Ary would have flushed with embarrassment when she saw Mr Derringer at his side if she were not so shocked by what was happening.

"Tripped, did you?" said the man, loud enough for the entire ballroom to hear. "I've been telling Lord Devenham these ten years at least to get his floorboards seen to, my gal. I went head over elbows into the fireplace last Christmastide. Burnt half me best wig, but saved the face."

He had reached them now, and stood leaning back on one leg, cane planted as if he owned the spot, and he was surveying Mr Roberts with a quizzing glass.

"Never mind, Roberts. Here." He handed him a lace-edged handkerchief. "Nothing a good laundress won't fix. Now, Mr Derringer, is this your delightful sister full grown?"

There was a general murmuring around the hall. While Ary was sure not all of the onlookers were convinced by this blustering gentleman's explanation of what had happened, the continuing scene was averted.

"Run along now, Roberts," said the old man in an undertone not meant to be ignored, "before I take it in mind to tell your father how much you lost to me at piquet Wednesday last."

Mr Roberts, whose sallow face had gone pink, whether from embarrassment or rage was uncertain, looked suddenly deflated by the threat. He mumbled something, handed back the older gentleman's handkerchief and then barely bowed before leaving.

Ary watched him go, dread creeping over her frame and stealing her breath. What had she done? She might have halted his words, but her actions would hardly stop the scandal now, they would cause the flames to burn hotter.

And was it true? Society had discovered her origins in the Foundling Hospital, but was what they said about her parents the rest of the truth? Was she not only poor, but disgraced as well? She was ruined. No longer a suitable companion for Charlotte, Mr Derringer would send her away. It was as she had always thought. Her life here was only temporary.

CHAPTER 16

"Well—what a to-do. Like your mother though, my gal," the older gentleman said to Ary. "She never could suffer fools either."

Mr Derringer introduced the man to Ary as Mr Pinchley—an old family friend who had been a university chum of his late father. He chatted amiably with Charlotte, telling stories of her and William as rascally children, and then turned once again to Ary.

"So, you have all the beauty of your mother then," he pronounced, puffing out his chest and taking a pinch of snuff as he surveyed her.

It wasn't the same lecherous gaze as Mr Roberts. Mr Pinchley appeared more like a benevolent grandparent. But the realisation that he might have known a mother she never had left her feeling hollow.

"I fancied myself half in love with Anne Goodwin as a lad. Calf-love it was—not that I knew it at the time." The man smiled ruefully. "She was a beauty, and spirited too—one couldn't help falling in love with the woman."

Mr Pinchley assumed Ary was this Anne Goodwin's daughter too.

"I think you may have mistaken me for someone else," Ary replied.

"Have I now?" Mr Pinchley took more snuff, looking between Mr Derringer and Ary. "Don't tell me you haven't told her, Derringer? Half the mamas here are talking of it."

"The timing hasn't been..." Mr Derringer trailed off, green eyes moving towards Ary, a sheepish expression on his face.

Did that mean there was truth in what she had been told?

"What is Mr Pinchley speaking of, William?" asked Charlotte, looking between her brother and the elderly gentleman.

"Dash it," Mr Pinchley said. "I see I've set the cat amongst the pigeons. Wasn't my intention. I thought you'd told her."

Flickers of indignation made their way through the shock Ary was in. If this was true—if she really was who they said she was—then Mr Derringer had known all along.

"I was sorry to hear about your mother, though I know it was years ago now. Your father too," Mr Pinchley said to Ary. "Never believed a word of what they said about him. Miss Goodwin had too much sense to shackle herself to a traitor."

A traitor? Is that what they said about him? Mr Pinchley spoke as if Ary should know. But she didn't know. She didn't know these people, nor the mother and father they spoke of. She had learned more in this short evening than she had been told in her entire life.

"Are you all right, Miss Giles?" Charlotte asked. "You look p-pale."

"I'm fine."

"The gal's shocked," Mr Pinchley said. "Best take her home, Derringer. Mrs Sade's on a crusade to let everyone in Society know the disgraced Anne Goodwin's daughter is back. And that wretch Mr Roberts was causing trouble along the same lines—if I'm correct?"

Ary half-nodded. A ringing had started in her ears, and it was growing louder.

"He was being ghastly," Charlotte whispered in horror at the memory, "saying the most awful things about Miss Giles' parents."

"While I understand dashing a drink over the buffoon's head, I don't think it helped your cause to be accepted into Society. You should have warned the girl, Derringer."

"Blast." Mr Derringer put a hand to his forehead, massaging the skin and letting out a frustrated breath.

Ary felt the indignation lighting her temper. She was being half-spoken to and half-spoken over. None of this was her fault, except that fracas with the drink, and it was getting more confusing and overwhelming by the second.

"Warned me?" Ary said. "I was unaware I was trying to be accepted into Society. I understood I was engaged as a companion to your sister, Mr Derringer." She stared at her employer who shifted uncomfortably.

"You owe the girl an explanation, my boy, but this isn't the place. It would have been better to announce her return to Society properly, but you were so determined to see her first. I just thought you'd have told her by now. Anyway, I'd take the girl home before she faints."

Ary shot Mr Pinchley a glare. "I have no intention of fainting."

To her irritation he chuckled. "Yes, that's the spirit I was talking about, and it's brought a bit of colour back into your cheeks."

"If we leave now it'll cause more talk," said Mr Derringer.

"I don't think you need to worry about that," Mr Pinchley replied matter-of-factly. "The rumour mills are already at work, and they have plenty to turn over."

Mr Derringer sighed. "Miss Giles, Charlotte, we should leave as Mr Pinchley suggests."

"I HAVE A HEADACHE," said Ary, hoping it would make her interview with Mr Derringer short.

They were alone in the study. Charlotte had been sent to bed when they arrived back at the Hall and Mr Derringer had requested Ary's presence here.

"I wish to explain."

"That I am the supposed daughter of Miss Anne Goodwin, a lady, and her common soldier husband who died in infamy?"

"Well..." Mr Derringer looked uncomfortable. "Yes."

"I hate to shatter whatever scandalous rumours have been circulating this evening, but I am not."

The carriage ride back to Duriel Hall had been plenty of time to consider her position. She had viewed her situation dispassionately in the chilly carriage and had come to the only logical conclusion.

They were wrong. All of them.

She was no more the daughter of a lady than she was part of their world. That was the stuff of orphans' dreams.

"But you are," Mr Derringer said, his deep voice gentle and his eyes willing her to believe him.

"I assure you, I am not. But if this misapprehension is going to cause issues for Charlotte's entry into Society then I will have to tender my resignation."

She had known it—that this happy situation could not last. It had been short-lived as all things were and soon she would be on her own again.

Mr Derringer was silent for several minutes. Jupiter, happy that his human companions were home again, was padding between them, wagging his tail, oblivious to the tension in the room. Aside from his panting, the only other noises were the clock on the side table ticking loudly and the crackling of the fire.

"I have something I need to show you," Mr Derringer finally said, seeming not to have heard her last words.

He went over to his desk and unlocked one of the drawers. He drew out an object and a letter and laid them on the leather top of the desk. Ary had been standing in the middle of the room, but the sight of that object drew her forwards. She stood and stared at it, eyes widening.

She glanced down to make sure that the wooden heart she always wore on her wrist was still there. It was. She looked again at the desk and saw an identical heart lying next to the letter. Then she looked up into Mr

Derringer's eyes, and with a feeling like a blow to her gut, she realised it was all true.

NONE of this had gone according to William's plan. Not the way she had found out. Nor Mr Roberts' behaviour. Not even Araminta herself. Now, while he watched her expression change as realisation dawned, he felt the worst kind of feeling. Guilt.

"I should have told you before," he whispered, watching as she picked up the second heart from the table and held it aloft.

"*MD* and *AG*," he said, "Mary Derringer and Anne Goodwin. Yours is the same, but the initials are reversed. Mary Derringer was my mother."

He picked up the letter from the desk and held it out to Ary. At length, her eyes moved from the heart to the letter, then to him. The distrust in them was evident. He winced at the sight of it.

Miss Giles placed the second heart back on the desk and took the letter from him. She began reading, still standing, but then he saw her sway a little. Finally, she slumped down into a chair, looking for the first time overwhelmed by the situation.

"I always thought the initials were for my father and mother," she said softly, the letter now forgotten in her lap.

He saw tears welling in her eyes as she stared at the carpet, the large drops falling down her face unheeded. He wanted more than anything to reach forward and brush them away. To ask for her forgiveness for keeping the truth from her.

"I've wondered who I am for so long." Her brow crumpled as she said the words, the tears now plentiful, falling down her face and coating her cheeks.

Her eyes flicked to his, tears ceasing. "You knew I was a foundling child all along?"

"Yes."

She emitted a hollow laugh.

"Here I was being careful not to reveal my shameful heritage, and you had the keys to it the entire time." She sighed again. "Why did you bring me here?"

"My mother," William explained. "She made me promise, before she died, that I would find you." He perched on the edge of his desk, folding his arms across his chest. "She was ashamed of leaving you in the Hospital when you were a child. She was frightened of the scandal. According to your mother's wishes, she ensured you were not renamed like the other children, and she ordered them to allow you to keep your mother's token as well as sending money for your education. But she said she had not done the one thing her friend had asked of her—invited you into her family."

He couldn't read the look in her eyes as he spoke, but now that he was telling her the truth, he knew he must not stop. He must get it all out and she could react as she saw fit.

"She never even met you for fear of... being connected with you." He grimaced at the coldness of that truth and the way Miss Giles flinched on hearing it. "At the end, my mother's memory was not what it was, and she could not remember the last place you had been living. I knew you had been left at the Foundling

Hospital and that my mother had sent money for your education.

"But when I went to the Foundling Hospital, they were less than generous in sharing their records with me," William carried on. "Mr Pinchley has long been a benefactor of the Hospital. He used his influence to persuade them to tell me where you had gone after your time there. That was how I found out you had been taken on by a charity school. I went there and spoke with Miss Drench, your old schoolmistress, and eventually she told me that my mother had arranged a position for you as companion to Mrs Stanaway, an old acquaintance of hers, at Edge House."

"But why would Mr Pinchley help you?"

"Well... " William wasn't sure it was his place to reveal the truth to Miss Giles, but he had already kept so much from her. "He was the man who was engaged to your mother when she eloped with your father."

She nodded dumbly, seeming as though she might break under the weight of these revelations.

"And it was safer for you to hire me as a companion to your sister, so that you might at any point dismiss me, should you find me wanting?"

"I did not know you," he said lamely, knowing that the Christian charity his mother had made him promise to show Miss Giles had been sorely lacking. "I wished to find out what sort of... who you were before I..."

He couldn't bring himself to finish. It sounded as callous out loud as it had begun to sound in his head since getting to know Miss Giles. "But even if you had been... I would not have left you without financial support. I would never have done that."

"You would have paid me off?" she asked, her

expression like stone. "Is that what you plan to do now you know who I am?" She rose from her chair, holding the letter in her hand still, her fingers tightening on the old paper. The light of defiance flashed in her eyes and her chin tipped up. "The girl who kicks improper gentlemen and dashes drinks over their heads."

"I don't hold any of that against you. Mr Roberts' behaviour was awful."

"I knew your kindness could not be genuine," Miss Giles carried on, like a frightened animal backed into a corner. "If a gentleman shows me any concern it is always in expectation of something. I had thought you were..." She trailed off and looked away from him.

A stab of remorse assailed him. Perhaps he was no different. What had he expected from her? He had been expecting her to prove her worth before he would offer the true familial love his mother had made him swear to. Unconditional love.

She rubbed her brow and sighed again.

"May I retire now?"

His brow raised. "If you wish."

"I am tired."

"Very well," he said reluctantly. "I will tell Charlotte the whole tomorrow morning."

Ary nodded and curtseyed to him.

He willed her to stay. He didn't want to send her away. He didn't want her to leave. Reaching out before he could stop himself, he lightly touched her forearm. The action surprised her into halting. She looked back at him, a question in her eyes. He wished to tear down the guard he saw there. To ask for forgiveness and tell her he knew who she was—kind, brave and fierce.

He saw the moistness on her lashes, the flush in her

cheek, his eyes falling on her barely parted lips. His gaze lingered there. He felt her arm move beneath his hand and cleared his throat awkwardly.

Stepping back, he released her. "Good night, Miss Giles."

She nodded, inclining her head, not showing any emotion on her countenance. Without a word she drew the study door shut behind her, and William moved over to where the fire burned low in the grate. Jupiter came to join him, not understanding the interaction that had just taken place, and pushing his wet nose into William's hand to persuade a stroke from his master.

William did as the animal bid him, unconsciously caressing the dog's head as he stared into the glowing embers, watching a flame or two licking lazily out of the ash, and considering what a mess he had made of everything.

*A*ry escaped into the garden after breakfast the following day. She inhaled the heady scent of the roses as she wandered further from the house, choosing paths that took her behind high rose bushes and yew hedges so she would not easily be found.

Today they were attending the Pump Rooms in Bath. Ary had heard about them during her time with Mrs Stanaway. They were a watering hole for the good and the great of Society. It was the last possible place she wanted to go after what had happened, but she did not have a choice—she was still employed by the Derringers.

She had managed a reasonable night's sleep after the revelations of yesterday, but this morning she had woken with a weight on her chest. It was an odd mix of feelings that enveloped her as she walked along the gravel path. A bittersweet happiness that she knew who her parents were now. A sadness to be reminded that she would never know them for herself. And then there was Mr Derringer.

Ary reached out to a rose as she passed, her fingertips

running over the velvet petals and the scent full and heavy creeping up to her nose. She was angry at him for sitting in judgement over her character, but the passage of the night had also brought with it perhaps a little understanding, even if she did not agree with his decision to keep the truth from her.

Ary had been wary of the Derringers in the first instance. She had not trusted them— not until they had proved themselves as kind and worthy people. Hadn't Mr Derringer simply done the same?

No. It was not the same. He had known about her past and chosen to keep it from her. But perhaps she could soften her heart towards him, knowing he had been protecting his sister until he knew Ary was a woman who would not hurt her or the family. Is that what he had decided? That she was worthy to know the truth?

No again. She had found out from Mr Roberts and Miss Sade. Ary shivered at the memory of their vicious words. Would Mr Derringer have told Ary the truth if his hand had not been forced?

Turning a corner, Ary followed another line of rose beds back to where an ornamental pond lay. She assumed that this morning she would be called to Mr Derringer's study, and he would do as he had implied last night—he would pay her off. She would be given an amount that would satisfy his conscience and she would be sent on her way.

Would she take it?

There was something within her which stopped her from being able to answer. It was a feeling she had not felt in her one-and-twenty years. A feeling of being where she was supposed to be. Duriel Hall. For all her attempts at viewing it as a transitory employment, the Hall had begun to feel like... home. If home was a place that one felt safe and cared for. And the Derringers, in spite of her best efforts, had grown on her. She cared for Charlotte.

Frowning, she wished she did not feel this weakness —this need for others. She knew it would do her no favours in the end.

"Araminta." Charlotte was coming along the path towards her.

Ary cleared her brow, not wanting to transfer her discontent to Charlotte, who had been nothing but kind to her.

"I looked for you at breakfast, but you did not come in."

Ary felt a stab of guilt, but there was no judgement in Charlotte's open countenance. The young woman came up to Ary and then hesitated, hovering before her awkwardly.

"How are you after l-last night?"

Ary wanted to assuage the look of concern on Charlotte's face, but did not know how to answer her. Her emotions were at war within herself and to explain them to someone else seemed impossible. The lack of an immediate response made Charlotte nervous.

"I-is it b-bad of me to have come?" Charlotte said, pressing her hands to her silk skirts repeatedly. "D-do you want to be al-lone?"

"Not at all." Ary broke into a smile, any vestiges of upset cleared away for Charlotte's benefit.

She stepped forward and took her charge's arm onto her own, turning to walk with her down the path. Ary might be in turmoil, but she had been employed to be a good companion to Charlotte, and that's what she would be. More than that, she liked this girl, and it was not her fault that Ary had been deceived, or that she might now be paid off and sent on her way.

The gravel crunched under their wooden heels as they walked in silence. Ary noticed the bird song, sharp and clear, carrying across the gardens to them.

"William has t-told me the whole," said Charlotte, her stammer still present, but her voice containing a more confident tone now Ary had reassured her. "I d-didn't know, and I'm so s-sorry that he did not tell you."

"It's not your fault," Ary said soothingly, squeezing Charlotte's hand which rested on her arm, but avoiding looking directly in the girl's eyes.

She knew it was not Charlotte's fault, but she couldn't be sure that her frustration wouldn't seep back into her expression.

"You must think us odious."

"Not you," Ary replied quickly. "No one could ever think you anything but the kindest woman." And Ary meant it. She felt a lancing pain in her heart at the sudden thought that she may not be Charlotte's companion for much longer.

"Oh good," Charlotte said, the stammer now disappeared, "because I was dreadfully worried you might go."

With her free arm by her side, Ary felt the wooden heart tap her palm as she walked. She grabbed hold of it.

"Only if Mr Derringer wishes to send me away." There, she had made her decision, she would stay unless Mr Derringer decided to pay her off and end her employment.

She took a deep breath. It had been easier than she had thought to decide.

"But William won't do that," said Charlotte, surprise and confusion mingled in her tone. "He told me you are to stay here and if you no longer wish to be my companion, then you shall be our guest, for as long as you wish to remain. This is your home now."

Ary sucked in a surprised breath. For some reason, this positive news caused a fresh lancing pain in her heart. What was the cause—the pain of hope? That she might have found a place she could stay and make her home? That Mr Derringer did not mean to pay her off and send her away—that he meant to follow through on his oath to his mother and provide Ary with a home?

"You didn't think we would just toss you out d-did you?" The stammer came back as the shocking nature of her question made Charlotte falter. "Your opinion of us m-must be very poor. I mean, I think William should have told you the truth—that was not the right decision on his part. But we would never wish you ill. William sees how you have been nothing but kind to m-me.

"I kn-now it must be frustrating with me st-stammering all the t-time, and you have been so patient. William likes it when people are kind to me. He once boxed one of his friend's ears when he made fun of me in our youth.

"And he said you're one of the most well-read women he knows. He says you are very quick at reading —quicker than him—and he prides himself on his reading. So for him to admit that... it's—"

The conversation was coming thick and fast from Charlotte, as well as these intimate details about Mr Derringer, which were knocking Ary's thoughts all out of order. Mr Derringer admired her? He was willing to allow her to stay and not as an employee but as a member of the household?

"And I had been so worried you would leave before my first assembly. It is at the Assembly Rooms in Bath and all of Society will be there."

Ary remembered all the eyes that had been on her last night.

"I am dreading it, to tell you the truth, and I will feel so much better with you there. You will go with me, now you are staying, won't you?"

Ary found herself promising to go before she considered any other answer.

"Yes, of course. I will not leave you to go alone."

But even as she said it, she knew that in going with Charlotte to the assembly Ary would be exposing herself to all those stares again. She would have to endure the wagging tongues of Miss Sade, Mr Roberts and countless others. But didn't she want to stay? She would have to bear it. Besides, now she had promised Charlotte, and she would not break her word.

"Splendid," Charlotte said beaming at Ary. "Now, William has called the carriage to take us to Bath—are you ready?"

Ary wasn't ready, but she allowed Charlotte to pull her back towards the house, and whatever fate that awaited her.

CHAPTER 18

William was waiting to take the ladies to Bath when Miss Giles descended the stairs into the hallway alone. It was a clear day, and the sun threw its beams through the east windows, piercing the old building with warm light, and illuminating sections of the opposite wall. She walked through the lines of light, the brightness causing her dark hair to shine and casting her features in a warm glow, before moving off her again, and leaving her in relative shadow.

She moved with such calm grace, in spite of the revelations of last night. William doubted he would be able to maintain such composure if he were in her position. Standing as he was, by the entrance to the Hall, she did not catch sight of him on reaching the bottom of the stairs. He should have said something straight away, or at least cleared his throat to draw attention to himself, but he didn't. He watched as she was drawn over to the archway that contained the carved words above. Her back was to him now. He saw her head tip up, her gaze no doubt tracing the stone lettering,

GOD IS MY HOME

He wished in that moment that he might read her thoughts. Was she considering who she was after yesterday's disclosures? Was she considering whether this could be her home after all she had learned? Did she think ill of him?

That last question is what had kept him up late last night. He had gone to bed a long time after she had left him. Even when he had eventually lain in bed, he found himself too agitated to stay there and had risen after only half an hour. He had paced about his room before lighting a candle and settling with a book that he forced himself to read until tiredness overcame his troubled mind.

He had been staring at her for several minutes now, intruding on whatever private moment this was. But he could not stop himself staring at her small, solitary figure as she looked up at the stone pediment over the entrance to the drawing room and contemplated its sentiments. William felt afresh his inadequacy after last night. He had done a poor job of explaining the truth to her and she had gone before he could tell her how bitterly he regretted his behaviour. More than that, he had not had the opportunity to tell her that he thought her one of the best women of his acquaintance.

Again, he did not think, if he were in her position, he would act in the same way. He had grown up in a loving family. It had been relatively easy for him to believe in a benevolent God and to become a gentleman in both name and character. But the deck of life's cards had been stacked against Miss Giles from the off, and yet she had not become a bitter person. Wary, yes—but not bitter.

William had seen her bow her head in prayer during the Sunday services she had attended with the family. Had she thought on the vicar's words last Sunday as William had? The clergyman had been preaching from the book of Acts. He had said that the Lord determines the time in which we will each live and the places we will inhabit.

That meant that William's bringing Ary here was not merely some benevolent plan of his dead mother's or his own—it was God-ordained. He felt, deep in his soul, that Miss Giles was supposed to be here—that she belonged at the Hall. In a few short weeks he had seen how she had cared for his sister and fitted into the household. He could not remember what it was like without her strong and calm presence here. When she had asked last night if he would send her away, nothing could have been further from his mind. The idea made his chest tighten.

The thought that she might be contemplating such a thing forced him to break in on her thoughts.

"Good morning, Miss Giles."

She turned, seeming to be half in her own thoughts still, and he realised with a start that she had tears on her cheeks. They were caught by the light, tracing shiny tracks down her face. He had not heard her crying.

"Oh," she said in a small voice. Her hands came up and she pressed gloved fingertips to her face, trying to wipe away the evidence of her emotion.

Her distress was a lance through William's heart. He had caused this with his selfish actions. Hastening to her side, he pulled a handkerchief from his pocket and handed it to her—the gesture feeling futile in the face of such emotion. He wished to offer her more. All the words he had not said last night. The comfort he had wanted to give her in her distress, but which he felt so inadequate to bestow.

As he stood closer he caught the faint scent of rose water. She was wearing a new dress, without the trimmed affectations of the most fashionable, in a deep green silk that set off her dark features and made William once again acknowledge her beauty.

As she reached out to take the handkerchief, her fingers grazed his. He stilled as they connected, wanting to prolong the touch, and her eyes darted up to his. He wondered how much she could read with those dark, steady eyes of hers. Could she read the sorrow he felt? Or the... attraction?

"I'm so sorry," he said, his voice low and husky.

Her hand disconnected from his and she pressed the handkerchief to her cheeks, her gaze falling from his.

"You have taken off your bracelet," he observed.

She halted, glancing down at her bare wrist and then brushing the fingers of her other hand against it.

"It did not seem an appropriate item of jewellery to wear anymore. Not in the present circumstances."

William stuck out his bottom lip unconsciously as he mulled on her words.

"It would be fitting to have it made into jewellery—the heart I mean—so that you could always carry it with you."

Miss Giles surprised him by breaking into a brilliant smile.

"With my vast fortune you mean?" The corner of her pink lips crooked up. "I do not think flaunting my heritage will do your sister any favours."

"It's part of who you are," William said fiercely. "I do

not think you have anything to hide or be ashamed of, and I don't believe Charlotte does either."

"That is kind," she said as if she were speaking to an angry child. Now her tears were dried, she tried to give the handkerchief back to him.

"Keep it," he said.

He was still standing close to her. Too close. But he wanted to be near this woman who faced life with such courage.

"We won't go to the Pump Room today. I will cancel the carriage," he said.

He turned away, not wishing to leave her, but unwilling to ignore her upset. Before he had gone two steps, he felt her hand on his arm. Stopping at the restraint, he turned back, looking from her hand to her face.

"No—please," she said. "We must go, for Charlotte's sake. Lady Amelia expects her. I will be fine."

His brow furrowed. How could she still be thinking of others after all that had occurred?

"It is not my sister I am concerned for in this moment. Charlotte may see her friends at another time."

He saw warring emotions on her face and then she said abruptly, "I don't understand..." She trailed off. Her brow puckered. She started again. "Your sister told me I will not be sent away. Why would you allow me to stay when you know I will cause gossip that will affect your family?"

Because all the gossipmongers in Society could go hang for all William cared. He turned to face her again. "Because it is the right thing to do."

Her expression made him think he had said the wrong thing.

"I... I was wrong to keep the truth from you." His words sounded lame even to his own ears. It was not enough. "And to think of sending you away after bringing you here... Please—"

His voice turned pleading. He hesitated a moment, and then did what he knew was improper but which he had desired to do for some time. He reached up and touched her chin, raising it so she would look him directly in the eye, his thumb running the line of her jaw. "Do not mistake my stupidity for callousness," he said slowly, enunciating every word, willing her to believe him. "This is now your home, for as long as you wish it, and we will never leave you alone again. Do you understand?"

He was unnerved to see fresh tears forming in her eyes. He could not seem to fix this situation. She blinked rapidly, half-shaking her head. He immediately dropped his hand.

"I don't expect you to forgive me for what I've done. You don't even have to speak to me, if you so choose. But you must know what I did not have the opportunity to say last night. I was wrong to judge you, but in doing so, I have found you to be one of the best women of my acquaintance. You have more courage, more sensibility and more intelligence than any lady I have met before—" He broke off mid-sentence, realising how much of his admiration he was revealing.

Miss Giles looked taken aback by his words. She remained silent. After a moment, she tried to hand back the handkerchief again. He responded by closing his hands over her own and shaking his head. Her hands were chilled under his. He wished to chafe them, to warm them. He felt a sudden urge to embrace her. The thought surprised him, and he stepped back just as the sound of a door shutting upstairs drifted down to them.

"Charlotte," he murmured.

Miss Giles nodded, smoothing her skirts, running fingers over her face again to erase any remaining tears.

"We do not have to go," said William.

"We must go," Miss Giles replied, avoiding his gaze. "For Charlotte's sake. I have promised her I will attend her first assembly at the end of the month. It will be as well if I have grown accustomed to whatever Society has to say by then."

He was floored by her resilience and found himself only able to nod in response. Charlotte descending the stairs precluded any further conversation, and Miss Giles was quick to go to his sister's side and walk out with her to the waiting carriage. They set off for Bath shortly after to face whatever Society would throw at them.

When they arrived at the Pump Room, William handed both ladies down from the carriage. Miss Giles stared up at the imposing classical facade and he caught a glimpse of what he thought was nerves in her dark eyes. She hid it as quickly as it had appeared and turned to take Charlotte onto her arm and enter the building.

A good selection of fashionable Society was scattered across the main room's floor. Some walked around in a slow circuit, chatting and sipping the waters. Older individuals sat at the edges on the few chairs provided. The classical lines, stuccoed décor and chandelier made no impression on William. He had been here countless times with his mother when she had been ill. If anything, this place evoked in him a moderate discomfort at the memories.

But he came for Charlotte's sake. While it was now growing more the haunt of the older and invalid members of Society, there was still a portion who came with said relatives, or for their own good health, to socialise at the famous Pump Room. It was the ideal place for Charlotte to come.

He saw Lord and Lady Arleigh on the far side, her ladyship in an animated conversation with Mr Pinchley. William had no doubt it was on horseflesh. Mr Pinchley bred his own and Lady Arleigh was reputed to have bought several. He spied Mrs Sade walking slowly around the room with her daughter. William grimaced. That meant Mr Roberts could not be far away as he always gravitated to her party.

There were a few ladies and gentlemen he did not know, no doubt recently arrived on the instructions of their physicians. Lord and Lady Mires were by the fountain procuring glasses of the famed water. Their daughter caught sight of Charlotte and waved.

"May we go, brother?" Charlotte turned eager eyes on him.

He nodded his approval and watched his sister and Miss Giles join the circuiting walkers, following the flow to where Lady Amelia stood. As soon as they reached her, William saw his sister strike up a lively conversation, and the moment Charlotte was settled, he saw Miss Giles' gaze wander.

She looked up at the chandelier, her eyes following the line of the ceiling, admiring the stucco William had ignored. Then her gaze drifted over the fine ladies and gentlemen present that he had only briefly surveyed. This was the world she should have been in, but it had been stolen from her.

William stepped out of the way of a promenading couple, bowing as he did so and offering a modest smile. He moved to the edge of the room, and found his eyes drawn back to Miss Giles. Her manner had changed. Her shoulders were high, there was faint colour in her cheeks and a look of discomfort in her eyes. What was she looking at? William followed her gaze to where Mrs Sade was now whispering to acquaintances. The woman kept looking over to Miss Giles conspicuously and her conspirators followed suit.

William ground his teeth, the muscles in his jaw flexing. He was just about to set off across the room to stand with Miss Giles and his sister, when he was hailed from another quarter.

"I didn't expect you here this morning, Derringer."

"Mr Pinchley." William reluctantly allowed himself to be waylaid. "I trust you are in good health this morning?"

"Well, I am not here for the waters if that is what you are implying." The older gentleman wore his old-fashioned bob wig, and had put a quizzing glass to his right eye in order to survey the room. "Rather, I am here to find out exactly what the rumour mills have turned out this morning."

"Oh?" William asked through gritted teeth.

"No need to look daggers at me, my boy—I'm not the enemy here."

William conceded and relaxed his shoulders a fraction. Pinchley had aided him in finding Miss Giles and supported her yesterday when facing Mr Roberts. The gossip was being promulgated from quite another quarter.

"I only wish I could do something to stop it."

"Aye," Mr Pinchley said with a sigh, allowing the quizzing glass to drop on its ribbon and gently bump against his rotund abdomen. "It would be fortuitous to be able to do so. However, if one could simply stop a scandal there would be many a peer who would attempt it. As you know, none are immune to the vicious overtures of Society's gossip, and it seems the mill is already twisting the truth."

William's chest tightened and his breath shallowed. How could it have gotten worse since only last night?

"According to some, the girl's father was no more than a common criminal, and others say she was born on the wrong side of the sheets."

William did not manage to stop the incredulous snort he emitted. "Absolute rubbish! Why people with small minds must need fabricate an entirely new and more scandalous heritage for Miss Giles is beyond me. She has done nothing to them."

He caught Mr Pinchley's wrinkled face creasing into a knowing smile, his pale grey eyes twinkling. "Beauty, Mr Derringer, will make the sweetest of us bitter with envy. Don't you see it?"

William felt the tips of his ears warm and dropped his gaze reluctantly from where it had been resting on Miss Giles and his sister across the room.

"Ah." Mr Pinchley's tone became as knowing as the expression on his face. "So, you have noticed." He retrieved his quizzing glass and set about spying Miss Giles in the crowd again. "I have already thought if I were thirty years younger... but alas, no. I was a scoundrel and a scapegrace in my youth and I shall be one in my aged state as well. I am not for the matrimonial state. If I was, I should have tried more earnestly to win Miss Giles' mother. But I can see you feel for the girl."

William did not answer. He was only just coming to terms with his feelings for Miss Giles himself.

"Rumours of her father mutinying in his regiment,

though—it's a bad business, and will not reflect well on yourself or your sister."

"She can do nothing to change what her father did."

"It was debated at the time," Mr Pinchley said, tapping the quizzing glass against his lips and looking up to the ceiling as he thought. "I remember there being conflicting accounts of his death—I had a friend working for the Northern Department of the Secretary of State at the time—something to do with disobeying the commanding officer's instructions to stay out of an inn near the town where they were stationed. Giles was supposedly one of the party who had disobeyed their commanding officer and then responded violently when they were found by a watch party. He was killed that night, but it wasn't clear whether Giles was there as their friend to round them up, or enjoying the local inn himself."

This was news to William. He had thought Miss Giles' father a common soldier who had died in disgrace, but his mother had not lived long enough to tell him anything further. Besides, she would not likely have known the truth. Those kinds of stories were not often spoken of in female circles.

"Regardless," William said, knowing he could not solve that mystery in this present moment, but he could aid Miss Giles now by being there to support her against these vicious rumours, "I should go and be with my sister and Miss Giles."

"You'll allow me to accompany you?"

Mr Pinchley didn't really appear to be asking as he was already moving off towards their destination.

"As you wish," William replied.

They walked together across the Pump Room,

cutting through the swathe of people circulating the room, making for Miss Giles. He was not sorry to have Mr Pinchley beside him. Judging from the hostile faces surrounding Charlotte, William would be glad of reinforcements.

CHAPTER 20

"I had thought, Miss Derringer, that your brother would not wish for you to be consorting with a woman of Miss Giles' family," Miss Sade said to Charlotte while Ary was off fetching glasses of the waters.

They were only a short distance from the fountain, and Ary could hear every word from the overloud Miss Sade.

"I d-don't think y-you s-should—"

"I'm sorry Miss Derringer, but I can't understand you."

A fire of indignation erupted in Ary's chest, and it took all her self-control not to discard the glasses and walk straight back to Miss Sade and give her a set-down. Not for what she had said about Ary, but for how she treated Charlotte.

"I'm only thinking of your wellbeing. My mama says her father was"—Miss Sade acted as though she meant to whisper the next bit, but she really did it so Lady Amelia and Mr Roberts, who were also in the circle, would lean in to listen—"a traitor."

Lady Amelia gasped. Mr Roberts' lip curled disdainfully.

"To be consorting with a woman of such—ill-breeding," Miss Sade carried on. "It is damaging, my dear Miss Derringer."

"I know I should consider myself exceedingly fortunate," said Mr Roberts. "To think I was taken by the girl at first—though I had come to think her too common for my tastes—and my instincts were right. Now we find out she is merely some chit born on the wrong side of the sheets to a bally traitor!"

Ary felt the aspersions like a lance through her heart. She had only just found out the truth about her parents and these people were already twisting it. They did not know her or her parents. They had no right.

"That is n-not—"

"I didn't know she was illegitimate," Miss Sade gasped, cutting across Charlotte again. Ary was not surprised that the woman was wholly taken in by the tales.

"Yes, and a low born father," said Mr Roberts. "I should have known with those looks. Pretty, yes, but in that vulgar way often seen among the common sort."

Ary had just come abreast of Mr Roberts and Miss Sade, standing with the glasses, gripping them so hard she thought they might shatter. They had not seen her yet.

"I heard her father died a traitor in His Majesty's army, a drunkard disobeying orders, and left her mother destitute. Charlotte, did you know about this?" asked Miss Sade.

"I hardly think the circumstances of her father's death are the concern of anyone here."

Ary's eyes snapped to where Mr Derringer had appeared at the opposite edge of the circle. He stood tall, his shoulders thrown back, a challenging look in his eye. Mr Pinchley was just behind him, his quizzing glass in play as he surveyed the group.

"He was a soldier who served King and country," Mr Derringer continued. "Which is more than any of us here can say. I believe that shows a man of more honour than a gentleman who thrusts unwanted attentions on ladies of their acquaintance, don't you Mr Roberts?" He enunciated the name, causing the circle to turn their gazes on the gentleman in question.

Miss Sade took a step away from Mr Roberts, bumping into Ary. A slosh of water fell over the rim of the glass and onto the floor.

"Oh, Miss Giles," said Miss Sade, pasting a false smile on her face.

"Thank you, I have just been waiting for the right moment to hand these over." Ary stepped forward and passed the glasses to Miss Derringer and Lady Amelia.

"Waiting?" Miss Sade flushed red.

"I believe she heard the same displeasing conversation that I have. Let me be clear," Mr Derringer said, "I engaged Miss Giles because she was qualified for the role and is the legitimate daughter of the late Miss Anne Goodwin, a friend of my mother. The fact that she is a lady of good character, admirable strength, and deep compassion, is only a benefit."

The group were silenced by Mr Derringer's speech. Ary's heart beat faster as Mr Derringer's words settled over her. He didn't have to do this. To take a stand for her. Other men would just let the cards fall where they may.

"Perhaps you wish to take a turn about the room with Lady Amelia," Ary suggested in hushed tones to Charlotte. The girl nodded nervously, finishing her glass and handing off to a waiter before disappearing with her friend, melting into the crowds.

"And will you do me the honour of accompanying me, Miss Giles?" Mr Derringer asked, offering his arm.

"Yes, thank you," said Ary, relieved to be leaving the situation she knew was not resolvable. The fire of gossip had taken hold and the buckets of common sense she and Mr Derringer were dashing over it were doing nothing to quench the flames.

"An excellent idea," said Mr Pinchley, "and I may talk with the formidable Miss Sade while you wander. It appears she has a firm grasp on the goings on in Society."

Ary doubted Mr Pinchley meant his words as a compliment, but she saw Miss Sade take it as such, smiling and fluttering her eye lashes at him. It was a clever move by the elderly gentleman, to prevent Miss Sade from attaching herself to Mr Derringer, but the supposed flattery only kept Miss Sade's expression sweet for a moment. As Ary turned away with her employer, she caught sight of a look passing between Miss Sade and Mr Roberts. It was one of malice and intrigue.

How much worse could they make it for her? Ary wasn't sure she wanted to find out.

"You needn't have done that," said Ary when they were across the other side of the room.

"It strikes me," Mr Derringer said pragmatically, "that speaking some truth would go a long way to quell the gossip. I should have told the truth in the beginning. All my silence has done is breed lies which are harming you."

Gratefulness washed over Ary. "I thank you for it," she said, pressing her fingers on his arm and realising how steady it felt beneath her touch.

She had not noticed until that moment that she was shaking. It was true, she was a courageous woman, or so she imagined herself to be, and she would never allow herself to be overset. That did not mean, however, that she enjoyed conflict, especially when she was at its centre.

"You thank me?" Mr Derringer asked incredulously. "I'd have thought you more likely to dash a drink over my head. It's what I deserve."

An involuntary chuckle bubbled up in Ary's chest and spilled out. He had just made a joke at Mr Roberts' expense whether he had intended to or not. She caught him glancing at her from the corner of her eye.

"I was angry you had not told me the truth," she said with sincerity, "but I can hardly blame you for the malicious proclivities of others—no matter how amusing I might find it to dash a drink over your head. It is my chosen way to deal with gentlemen I find disagreeable."

"And highly effective I should think."

"It has not failed me yet."

Ary was surprised at the ease with which they spoke. Something about the way he had defended her had formed a bridge of trust between them.

"I am sure half the women in Society are jealous that you had the nerve to throw a drink over Mr Roberts' head, which is likely what they have fantasised about numerous times."

They had walked a slow circuit of the room and were now into their second. Ahead of them Charlotte and Lady Amelia were walking arm in arm and chattering to one another.

"I shall say nothing to that," Ary said, but she couldn't help her smile coming back.

"It's good"—Mr Derringer hesitated—"to see you laugh."

It was such an intimate observation that Ary felt a sudden warmth wash over her. She had never been so keenly observed before—at least, not positively. They walked a few steps in comfortable silence. The back of Ary's neck prickled. Without the distraction of Mr Derringer's own conversation she began to notice once again the eyes that followed them around the room.

"You need not do as you did just now. If you defend me it will only cause more talk which will hurt your family. I can defend myself."

She felt Mr Derringer's arm stiffen.

"It is doing your sister's entrance into Society no good."

Which was why she had to leave. No matter the ease with which she spoke to this man now, nor the security she felt when she was in his presence. She could not cause harm to another. Even now, she knew that despite Mr Derringer's best efforts, rumours about Ary were swirling and her name was entangled with that of her charge. She had promised to stay until the assembly, but no longer, and now she wasn't sure if she should stay until then.

"I own it is not ideal, but you are part of our household now—a part of the family. I should have presented you as such from the outset."

Family. A wave of emotion crashed over Ary. It left her drenched in bitter sweet sadness. She had never been called part of a family before. Yet her very presence hurt this family. She felt unwanted tears pricking her eyes and threatening to jump overboard.

"But I can't be," Ary said, barely above a whisper. "Not when it causes such trouble. Besides, you barely know me. How can I be part of a family when only a letter written years ago connects us?" Her voice broke over the words and she felt the first of the tears escape down her cheek.

She wanted more than anything in the world for Mr Derringer to tell her she was wrong and an immovable part of their family. To fight for her and overcome all the misgivings she felt. Was that selfish of her?

"You're crying," he said, halting, looking down at her, eyes wide with concern.

The gazes he gave her were becoming increasingly hard for her to withstand. They released emotions in her she neither wanted to face nor acknowledge.

"I must take you home. We should not have come."

Ary scrubbed away the tears and looked defiantly up at him.

"I apologise, Mr Derringer. I shall be all right in a moment. Forgive me." She pulled the handkerchief he had given her earlier from her pocket and discreetly dabbed at her face. "Perhaps I might step out for a few minutes. The fresh air will help me."

At that moment Charlotte and Lady Amelia came back to ask William if they might go to Milsom Street. While they accosted him for the answer they desired, Ary slipped unnoticed from the Pump Room and away from Society's judgemental eyes.

CHAPTER 21

Ary sucked in another lungful of air and walked further down the street, away from the Pump Room's entrance.

The sun was high by now and the haze of the morning sufficiently burnt off to make it a warm autumn day. The Bath stone had shrugged off its sad grey for a warm natural colour and the happiness of the weather had transposed itself upon the pedestrians and street hawkers.

There were the sounds of greetings and laughter, everyone going about their days, knowing their place in the world and their purpose in the day. Ary had never had that. When she had been young, it had been about her days in the Foundling Hospital. The never-ending cycle of prayers and mealtimes, school lessons and sewing, kitchen tasks and hymn singing. Even Mrs Stanaway had a set routine which Ary had been under pain of death to abide by. The structure of the day had always been there—and she had not had the time to think ahead.

Since coming to Duriel Hall she had been afforded the time to consider her future. More than that—the revelations of her heritage were making her consider it in ways she never had before. Could she really have a permanent home with the Derringers? Mr Derringer seemed to think so. Perhaps Duriel Hall was not destined to be just another in a series of places she slept. Maybe now she could consider more than getting through the day before her—she could look to the future.

But if she allowed herself to think like that, what security was there in it? She could already sense the anxious feelings that accompanied such thoughts. After all, she was not a blood relation of the Derringers. They had each other when the world turned against them. Ary had no one.

"I don't care what he says, she's an ill-bred wench and not a fit companion for Miss Derringer."

Ary heard Mr Roberts' nasal voice before he came into sight. She was standing beside a shop doorway and retreated further into the shadows when she heard him.

"I certainly wouldn't have her as a companion for my daughter," said Mrs Sade, "and I can tell you for certain, my child, I shall not have you associating with Miss Derringer if they are insistent on keeping that woman in their employ."

"I shouldn't like to see her anyway, Mama. You needn't worry about keeping me away from her," Miss Sade said in a disdainful tone.

"Bravo!" came the sycophantic voice of Mr Roberts.

"To think her father a traitor, though Mr Derringer..." Miss Sade trailed off. There was a thoughtfulness to her tone now.

They were drawing nearer, and Ary turned into the

corner of the shop doorway so they would not see her face. She hoped beyond hope that they would pass by without noticing her. Their voices grew louder.

"Have no fear, Miss Sade," Mr Roberts said. "The charms of the common are not long lasting. Why, I am proof of it. I thought her a nice enough gal but soon tired of her and I was right to do so. No doubt I sensed it."

"Oh, well," Miss Sade said, growing flustered. Ary realised with embarrassment that they were implying Mr Derringer held her in affection, and that Miss Sade was jealous of the fact.

The idea that she was causing yet more talk made the sick feeling in Ary's stomach worsen. Yet, the idea that there was any truth to what they said of her charming Mr Derringer, made her feel... she hardly knew.

"I will not speak of my feelings," Miss Sade said in a teasing voice and Ary could just imagine the face she was pulling to go with the tone. "But Mama is right—"

They had just passed the doorway in which Ary stood and now their voices were fading. "We must cut Miss Derringer until her brother sees sense and removes Miss Giles from his family's employ."

Ary felt sick. They were talking about damaging Miss Derringer's entry into Society through no fault of the girl's. No. It was Ary's fault. She had been born to a poor father and a disgraced mother.

"I shall tell Lady Mires as much," Mrs Sade continued. "Her daughter is entirely too familiar with the Derringer girl. Who knows what effect a woman of Miss Giles' character might have on both of them? No self-respecting mother would put her child at such risk."

Now they would take away Charlotte's dearest friend. Ary could not let this happen.

Their voices became indistinct after that, mixing with the street's noise until Ary could hear them no more.

She gripped the railings beside her, breathing in deeply through her nose. She forced herself to remain calm and push away the feelings of nausea. Any vestiges of uncertainty faded, and in the cold hard light of reason she knew only one option was open to her. To protect Charlotte, even Mr Derringer, she could not stay. She needed to go where she was not known. Where her mother was not remembered, and her father's traitorous figure cast no long shadows. She must leave Duriel Hall.

WILLIAM WAS unable to travel directly home with his sister and Miss Giles after visiting the Pump Room. He had business to attend to in Bath and sent them home in the carriage, ordering the driver to return for him in the afternoon. It was not what he wanted. When he had seen the anxiousness on Miss Giles' face as they left the Pump Room, he had told her all would be well. That she need not worry over the ignorant words of a few individuals in Society. But her expression had not changed, and he had reluctantly watched her enter the carriage with his sister and drive away.

Her expression haunted him as he walked through the Bath streets, leaving the classical architecture of the Pump Room and the colonnaded walkways behind, and making his way south towards the river Avon. Turning west he came on to Corn Street and a short way along entered one of the buildings, his attention finally moving from Miss Giles to the task at hand.

He found the jewellers his family had patronised for the past several decades largely unchanged within. It was still decorated in the Rococo style of the forties. There were opulent scroll motifs on the edges of the ceilings and over each doorway. The furniture was heavily gilded, with gold framed mirrors hanging at intervals along the walls, the latter were decorated in pastel colours of blue and pale pink.

William was greeted soon after entering and taken to a room at the back of the building where his mother's jewels—the emerald earrings and necklace—were laid out on a velvet cushion, sparkling from their recent clean.

"Thank you," said William, addressing the jeweller who rose from behind the desk to greet him.

The gentleman shook William's hand, his bewigged head bobbing along with the movement, and then he placed the items in their travel case, turned the key and handed it to his client.

"I am sure your sister will look very becoming in them."

William agreed. They had been cleaned for that exact purpose as a surprise for Charlotte to wear at her first assembly, planned for the end of the month. She would be pleased to wear something of their mother's. Perhaps by then the gossip surrounding Miss Giles would have died down.

Taking the case from the older gentleman, William

was about to turn and leave when he bethought himself of the idea that had come to him that morning.

"I had thought to commission something."

The jeweller's ears pricked up, his eyes sparkling at the prospect. William began to explain the image he had conjured in his mind's eye, and the man soon grew excited. Fetching a sheet of foolscap and a piece of charcoal, the jeweller began sketching as William spoke.

"Yes, that's it," said William, coming around the desk and looking down at the finished drawing. "How long do you suppose it might take to make it?"

The older gentleman tapped the charcoal to his face, leaving an unconscious black mark on the cleft of his chin.

"It is the stones that will take time to arrive. I shall have to order them from London. I expect I may have it done in less than two weeks."

William's eyes were still rapt on the paper, following the lines of charcoal in their large sweeps until they collided in a single sharp point. Two weeks. That would suit.

"Yes," he said, in a thoughtful voice. Then he looked up, a visage of resolution. "Please consider it commissioned. May I take the sketch?"

"Of course—just let me ask my apprentice to copy it out for you." The jeweller called through to the front of his shop and soon the boy—the lad of fifteen or sixteen who had shown William in—appeared and copied out the drawing with a neat, precise hand.

With that piece of paper folded and nestled in his breast pocket, and his mother's jewel box beneath his arm, William headed straight home.

His spirits rose. Telling the truth was the first step in

ensuring Miss Giles could take her place in Society. They had met with challenge, that was true, but William felt a rush of hope that perhaps it was not so insurmountable after all. They had to stay the course, and he had faith it would turn out well in the end.

CHAPTER 22

William watched Miss Giles descend the stairs of Duriel Hall in her new cerulean blue dress for the assembly. It had been three weeks since the episode in the Pump Room. In that time they had attended several gatherings and the gossip surrounding Miss Giles had grown worse.

In this present moment, however, William forgot all about it. The colour of Miss Giles' dress made her already dark eyes impossibly darker. Deep enough for any man to get lost in. Her hair was dressed slightly differently too—piled high on her head in curls and waves, powdered according to the latest fashion. Around her neck was a ribbon matching the blue of her dress, and another was threaded through the waves of her hair. He imagined pushing his fingers through that hair, slipping his hands down her neck and stroking the smooth pale skin.

William caught himself, squeezing his hands into tight fists until the skin was taut over his knuckles. He willed himself to ignore Miss Giles' attractive features.

But it was impossible. From the fine waist to the pale décolletage, from the soft Cupid's bow of her upper lip to the dark, mesmerising eyes above. He had known she was attractive when he first laid eyes on her, but the woman he saw before him now was beautiful.

It wasn't just her appearance that had William's chest tight with longing. It was that beneath that pale skin beat a heart of steady courage. Within those deep eyes was a woman of integrity and honour. The delicate shoulders dressed in that cerulean dress had carried more of life's weight with dignity than any other woman of William's acquaintance. He had been brooding on the character and beauty of Miss Giles ever since his outburst in the Pump Room two weeks ago.

When he had spoken those words—'good character', 'incredible strength and compassion'—he had been struck with how true they were, and how he had never before met a woman of Ary's calibre.

She arrived at the bottom of the stairs and William unballed his fists to take her hand and bow over it. Despite the smallness of her hand within his, she held his firmly. With the same courage with which she faced all of life, it seemed.

"Good evening, Miss Giles." Her name almost caught in his throat. What was wrong with him? He felt like a schoolboy before a pretty girl, not a gentleman on the edge of thirty. "You are looking very beautiful this evening."

He meant to speak the compliment lightly. It was, after all, objectively true. But the words came out deep and husky and with as much feeling in their tone as a lover might have at a secret tryst.

He was still holding her hand. In truth, he wished to

keep hold of it and lay a kiss upon its back. He pursed his lips and dropped her hand. At the moment he did, his gaze lifted from where it had been hovering on her chin and he caught her eyes. They were wide with speculation, her arched brows raised in query. He took a step away, hoping the proximity was what caused this temporary insanity.

"Miss Derringer will be down shortly," Miss Giles said, in an emotionless voice.

"Shall we wait in the drawing room? There is a fire in there," said William—though he did not feel the least need for warmth. Since the moment he had set eyes on Miss Giles in her blue dress he had felt waves of heat continuously rolling over his body and they did not seem inclined to abate.

Miss Giles nodded. He offered his arm, looking forward to the feel of her hand on it again, and they entered the drawing room together.

It was a clean and uncluttered room. Unlike the cosy sitting room that was for family, this room was kept for entertaining guests. He wondered if Miss Giles had been in here before. It was usually reserved for morning calls, but they had not received any of late, as they had been paying the calls themselves. Miss Giles walked around the room, looking at every piece of furniture, at every painting.

She glanced at him surreptitiously and he soon realised she was not interested in the room. She was avoiding his gaze. Had he been so transparent?

"Still no token?" he asked, looking overtly at her wrist in the hopes he might hide his patent admiration.

"It's in a safe place," Miss Giles said, hand moving unconsciously to her bare wrist.

William thought of the object that the jewellers had delivered to the Hall earlier today. It was locked safely away in the desk of his study. Should he get it now?

"This evening is about Charlotte. I have no wish to detract from her with my less than salubrious heritage."

William noted the smile Miss Giles forced upon her face. There was no humour there. He thought better of fetching the item.

"Your actions should not be dictated by other people's small minds," he said, a hint of peevishness in his voice, knowing he was being hypocritical. If he really believed that, he would fetch the jeweller's creation now.

"I'm not sure you fully appreciate the damage I'm causing."

"Not you." He strode forward and took her upper arms in his hands, his grip firmer than he intended. "You are not the cause."

"At the risk of angering my employer—I must disagree."

He released her abruptly and exhaled harshly.

"Have you always been so stubborn?" he asked, half-provoked and half-amused.

He was torn between shaking the despair from her and kissing it away with his mouth. Gracious! He was losing all control.

"Miss Drench used to say so."

Here was another pearl of truth she was sharing freely. They were so rare he treasured each one of them as they were revealed. Turning away, exhaling slowly this time, he looked into the fire. When he felt her gentle touch on his arm he tensed, swinging around to find her right beside him, those dark eyes staring up at him open and unguarded.

"You do not need to worry about me," she said.

He was staring at her lips as she spoke, but then the light of sadness in her eyes arrested him.

"I've been at my happiest here at Duriel Hall. You have been very kind to me—you both have—and I should never wish to harm either of you."

The earnestness in those eyes pulled at his heart so hard he found himself forgetting to breathe. They stayed like that, staring at each other, neither willing to move on from this moment.

Then the door opened, and Charlotte entered. She paused on the threshold and when William and Miss Giles saw her they stepped apart. The moment was gone and now they must face Society.

CHAPTER 23

"William," said Charlotte, drawing him from the lingering gaze he had on Miss Giles.

They were only halfway through the evening at the assembly, and the time had dragged. Perhaps it was the brief looks of discomfort he caught on Araminta's face whenever she noticed the stares. It made the gathering, which was supposed to be a joyful social occasion, feel like purgatory. He hated to see Miss Giles' discomfort, and as much as he had told her not to concern herself with tittle tattle, he could see Society was very much concerning itself with Araminta Giles.

"William," his sister said again.

"Sorry—yes Lottie?"

His sister had enjoyed a few dance partners, but William had noticed her shortage of suitors. Ary had been correct about the damage.

"You w-will forgive me, I hope, for saying so."

It was unusual for her to stammer with him. He

removed his attention from where Araminta was speaking to Mr Pinchley and rested his gaze on his sister.

"I think you care for Miss Giles."

William felt a shiver of embarrassment run through him.

"I care for her wellbeing, yes, as the daughter of mother's friend."

"No," said Charlotte, her voice gaining confidence. "I mean—I think you love her."

A wave of shock rolled over William. He opened his mouth to speak but no words came out. To his chagrin, he saw Charlotte break into a grin.

"I thought so," she said, all stammering gone.

"What?" The word broke off in his mouth like a twig. To anyone who wasn't family it was a warning of his mood. Charlotte may have been nervous to bring up this outrageous subject, but now it was out, and she believed him cornered, she had turned into a teasing sibling.

"She *is* lovely—everyone can see that."

"Yes, but admiring someone is hardly the same as being in love," he said in his best big brother voice.

"I know," said Charlotte, rising to his tone and crossing her arms impatiently. "But you do more than admire her. I've never seen you stare so much at a woman, or give her access to your books, or protect her honour."

William felt himself colouring and ground his teeth, willing the blood to drain from his neck and cheeks.

"Charlotte, stop it."

"I'm right." She ceased her arm-crossed battle-stance and began to clap her hands. "I'm right, I'm right! Ary will make a wonderful sister, and just think how happy Mama and her friend would have been."

"Charlotte!" William whispered in shocked accents, turning on her and grabbing both her hands to still them. "Someone will hear you."

"I am right then?" she asked, her green eyes sparkling mischievously at him. They matched her mother's jewels, the emerald necklace shining bright against her pale skin.

William did not respond. Having stilled his sister's attention-drawing outburst, he turned back to surveying the room serenely as any other ball attendee might. Pretending his sister had not just struck the truth of what he had been realising himself.

"It's not that simple," he said quietly after a few moments.

"According to who?"

The question made him fall silent again. He opened his mouth to offer a quick rejoinder, but none came.

"It strikes me, from my short time in Society," Charlotte said, taking on the voice of an aged sage, "that Society makes a great deal of things which aren't really a great deal at all. Araminta is a daughter of the quality, and you are a gentleman. I know her father was a common soldier, but her mother was a lady. I don't see a problem."

His sister's simple words echoed around William's mind. Was it that simple? But even with the fears over what Society might say, what of Ary? What did she think? How could he show her he could be trusted after all he had done to her? If he proposed, he was not certain the answer would be the one he wished for. He had seen the mirroring desire in her eyes when he thought to kiss her in the library, but so much had happened since then, and those dark eyes were still a mystery to him. He could not be sure whether she returned his regard. Whether she even wished to be around him.

Besides, he did not want to force her to accept his suit through need. No, that would be the worst thing. After all the choices that had been taken away from her in life, he did not wish to take this choice from her as well. He wished her to be free. Free from the gossip, free from the aspersions, and free from the strictures her situation had put on her life.

No, he could not tell her of his feelings, even if they were solidifying. He needed instead to show her that Duriel Hall was her home now regardless. That there was no obligation upon her. More than that, he needed to try and stop the fires of scandal that were taking hold across Society. He had an idea.

"Charlotte?"

She turned to him expectantly.

"You know when we used to pass around secret messages? Well, I have one for us to pass around this ballroom, except it won't be a secret—we shall only pretend it is."

"Why?" Charlotte asked.

"Because when people think something's a secret they pass it along much faster."

"And what is this secret—that is not a secret—which you wish to pass on?" asked Charlotte, her eyes beginning to dance.

"The not-secret will tell the truth of Miss Giles' past. Are you with me?"

"Oh yes, William—let's." She looped her arm through his and they set out around the dancefloor, their first target the redoubtable Mrs Sade.

IT WAS AMAZING how intently people listened and how quickly they passed the information on, when you told them it as if it were the latest *on dit*. William and Charlotte had made quick work of the ballroom. Apparently people were as keen to speak to them as they were to tell the truth about Ary. The truth of her mother and father, of their love for one another, and their care for their daughter. That he had died in service to his country and that Mr Pinchley did not believe the scandal surrounding his death. That his widow had been forced to give up their child to the Foundling Hospital and that it had been Mrs Derringer's dying wish to see the child found and restored to the Society she had been taken from.

The thing was, the truth had all the makings of the best gossip—star-crossed love, dying for your country, and the redemption of a child. Everyone who heard the tale could not help but be enthralled by it and repeat it to their acquaintances.

What William and Charlotte had not counted on, however, was that nothing spreads faster or more virulently than stories of tragedy and shame.

"But how can one be sure?" asked one middle-aged gentleman who had made the Derringers' acquaintance a few months ago. "What is it they say—no smoke without fire?"

William had been explaining the truth of Miss Giles' heritage and her father's innocence for the past five minutes.

"Yes, indeed—that is the thing," said his wife, a

pleasant enough woman who had the unfortunate ailment of being an echo of her husband's often loudly proclaimed views.

William gritted his teeth. It was individuals like this gentleman who would promulgate the gossip surrounding Miss Giles.

"I feel for the lady—woman, that is," the wife carried on, glancing nervously at her husband before prattling on faster and faster as though her words were running down a hill, "for I am sure she cannot help her character, being so connected with that of her father—"

"I do not think there is as much innocence there as you say," said Mrs Dibley, a local vicar's wife whom William had unfortunately met several times in the past. "I have spoken to the girl and there was something about her I could not warm to."

William was about to snap at the woman's inference when he felt his sister's gloved hand pressing on his forearm.

"Yes." The other woman was swayed just as easily by Mrs Dibley's words as she was by her husband's. "It really is too bad, being a traitor to the country. Society can hardly forgive it."

"Indeed it cannot," said Mrs Dibley, shaking her plump face vigorously and not noticing the look of thunder on William's own.

"That's right!" said her husband, chiming back in. "What would that make of us? To accept such dastardly behaviour? It makes a mockery of the military service, and just shows you the kind of blood the gal has running in her veins."

"I have a-always thought Miss Giles t-to have exceptionally good c-character," said Charlotte.

William felt the red mist which had been descending across his vision lift a little.

"She is," he managed to grind out, irritated that he could think of nothing more powerful to say. Nothing polite at least.

"I'm sure *you* think that," said Mrs Dibley, directing a condescending gaze at Charlotte.

"Can't tell though, can you?" the man cut in. "Perhaps she's as dissembling as that father of hers. Though of course, I don't blame you for wanting to help the gal," the man blurted out when he finally caught sight of the look in William's eyes.

"Of course not," said Mrs Dibley in a sycophantic voice, "you are both simply good-hearted just as my husband the vicar has said before."

William said nothing. It was rude, but this conversation was pointless, and he wished it to end. He was more than willing to speak to those who would listen to reason. These people were not reasonable. They had made up their mind about Miss Giles and there would be no dissuading them, no matter how wrong they were.

The couple made some excuses about going into the supper room and Mrs Dibley mercifully left with them to go in search of her husband. Though she did not leave before saying how she hoped Mr Dibley might have occasion to visit Duriel Hall in the future.

"That did not go as w-well as I'd hoped," Charlotte said in a glum tone.

"Fools."

His sister didn't say anything in response but instead looked about her. "Where's Miss Giles?"

"I believe she is conversing with Mr Pinchley over there." William gestured to the other end of the oblong room. At least this time Miss Giles had not overheard the conversation concerning her.

"Do you think they will see it—the truth I m-mean?" asked Charlotte.

"Only time will tell," said William, struggling to hide his disappointment. "At least our dearer friends listened to us."

But had they believed them? That was the real question, and in all truth, William wasn't sure of the answer.

"We have to hope that time will encourage this to blow over."

Time might be their only ally, for it seemed to William that no matter how much they doused the flames with common sense, the fire burned hotter. He feared that the story of Miss Giles' father being a drunk and disobeying orders, mutinying against his superiors and dying in ignominy, was too tantalising not to repeat.

William and Charlotte continued their crusade on Miss Giles' behalf, but as the evening wore on, William grew disillusioned. He recognised people's expressions— even those of their close friends—for what they were. Expressions of sympathy towards the brother and sister whom they believed had been taken in by falsehoods. They thought he and Charlotte were too good, and did not blame them for wanting to believe the best of Miss Giles. Instead they pitied them that their charity case was no more than the ill-bred daughter of a traitor.

The hope he had set out with when he and Charlotte had determined to tell the truth had shrunk under the cynical gaze of Society. Now he was not so sure his plan would work.

This fear was brought home when Mrs Sade, her

daughter and Mr Roberts arrived at the assembly. Whatever dampening of the gossip William and Charlotte had managed seemed to be undone. Whispers, glances and outright cuts besieged them on every side.

When they eventually left, William noted Miss Giles was quieter than usual. Even when Charlotte tried to engage her in conversation on their return journey to Duriel Hall, Miss Giles said little, claiming tiredness. But it was not only weariness that marked her countenance. No, it was sadness and William ached to see it.

CHAPTER 24

Charlotte and Miss Giles were late to rise the next day, so William missed seeing them at breakfast. Arriving back at the Hall late morning after attending to some estate business, he found his sister attempting a watercolour in the garden. Miss Giles was reading in the rose drawing room, the French doors open onto the artist at her work, and Jupiter on the rug, his head resting on Araminta's feet.

"*The Odyssey*—an epic read, Miss Giles," he said lightly, looking over her shoulder at the tome in her hand, "and a scandalous one for a young lady."

She jumped when he spoke, but he was pleased to see a small smile appear on her lips shortly after.

"Epic indeed," she said, half-closing the book and giving a soothing stroke to Jupiter who had been upset by her movements.

"I couldn't stand it as a boy," he said, taking a nearby chair and stretching his legs out, hoping his relaxed pose would do something to encourage her to relax herself.

"They made us read it out at school, right up until Odysseus makes it home to his Penelope."

"I haven't got there yet," Miss Giles scolded, a frown on her fine brow. "I didn't know Odysseus made it home."

"Oh." He reached up to cover his mouth. "I am sorry."

And then the most wonderful thing happened. She began to laugh. But it wasn't that light and practised tittering of the ladies of Society. No. It was a belly-deep gurgling laugh that came up and rolled joyfully out.

"Are you bamming me?" William asked, his hand dropping from his mouth and pounding the chair arm demandingly.

Miss Giles' infectious laughter was getting to him. He felt an answering sound rumble up from his chest.

"It was too tempting," she said, laying the book aside and reaching up to dab at her eyes. "Who doesn't know that Odysseus gets home in the end?"

"Well," said William, leaning back in his chair and shrugging his shoulders. "I haven't met many young ladies who read ancient poetry in their leisure time."

"Then the ladies you know are missing something wonderful, even if it is improper."

William thought *she* was rather wonderful, and all others missed being her.

"I am glad you are here," she said, her tone turning serious. "I wish to thank you for the use of your library, and to tell you that I am sorry to be resigning from my role as Charlotte's companion."

The words, delivered so quickly after such a precious moment, hit William like a blow to the gut. The reassurance over her situation he had been planning to say died on his lips. The colour drained from his face and all he could do was stare at her.

⁓ • ⁓

ARY LOOKED AWAY, hating to see the shock in Mr Derringer's eyes.

"But why?" he asked, in a tone that suggested she had wounded him with her words.

She had thought he would be relieved. His obligation to her would be at an end now she had found other employment. She steeled herself again. Smoothing her skirts she looked back at him calmly as she spoke.

"I promised Charlotte I would stay until her first assembly. That has now passed, and I have found a new position in Yorkshire—as governess for a friend of Mr Pinchley's." She paused, willing herself to stay calm. "I think it is for the best."

She gestured out the open doors to Charlotte who was measuring a stone urn in the distance with the handle of her paint brush. "My presence will no longer detract from Charlotte's coming out in Society. You saw what happened last night. This way you will no longer be burdened by me—"

"Burdened?" He cut her off and to her surprise he looked angry. "I am not burdened by you. Neither of us are. I told you—this is your home now for as long as you wish it to be."

"I've caused enough trouble."

Mr Derringer leapt from his chair causing her to inhale sharply. He began pacing before her.

"Pinchley shouldn't have done that," he said, raking

a hand through his unpowdered hair, loosing a lock of it from the green ribbon.

"He was only helping." Ary had expected disappointment, but not this. Mr Derringer's reaction was stronger than anything she had supposed.

She wasn't oblivious to the way he had been looking at her, but she had told herself it was concern over her welfare. In this moment she was not so sure. Those doubting feelings were dangerous though, and she pushed them away.

"It's for the best," she repeated in her calm tone, hoping to placate him.

With Ary gone there would be no one to cause talk. When he realised it would be a blessing for Charlotte and himself, surely he would come around. She was being rational. Mr Derringer was not.

But instead of her words soothing him, as she had hoped, they seemed to do the opposite. If anything, his pace sped up, and the hand he was repeatedly raking through his hair became more erratic.

She pushed back a sudden overwhelming desire to take the words back. To rise from her seat and take his hands to still them. He could not see it now, but he would in time—it was impossible for her to stay.

"It's one thing for me to be the daughter of a lady who married below her station," said Ary, feeling the need to explain her decision if only in another attempt to calm Mr Derringer. "But for my father to be a traitor, and to have died in such circumstances—it is shameful. I cannot allow you to be damaged by associating with me."

The words felt difficult to form and pronounce. She had allowed herself to become attached to this place, to these people, and she had told herself even after the truth of her heritage came out that she might be able to stay. But she could not. She did not belong here, and no matter how much she would miss Charlotte, and the peculiar tugging within her chest when she thought of seeing Mr Derringer no more, she could not be the cause of another's pain.

"I disagree," said Mr Derringer, ceasing his striding and turning upon her. "This is your home now. We are not just your employers, we are your—" He hesitated, but then resolve showed in his eyes and he said with conviction, "Family."

The words which Ary had been waiting for her whole life hit her so hard in the chest that a soft unbidden cry escaped her. She clamped her hands over her mouth, but it did nothing to stop the tears which came fast, rolling down her cheeks and then onto her fingers.

"Ary!" Mr Derringer gasped, striding over and kneeling before her to take her hands in his.

The sound of her nickname on his lips was too much. A fresh wave of tears spilled over.

"Don't you understand? You belong here now—at Duriel Hall—with Charlotte and me."

It was Mr Derringer who didn't understand. He didn't know what it was like to be outside of the Society into which he had been raised. He didn't understand the risk he was taking for Charlotte and himself. But Ary knew what those judging eyes felt like. She had felt the harsh lash of the gossipmongers' tongues, and known the isolation of not belonging.

"Stop it," she whispered, allowing the tears free rein down her cheeks. She took command of her emotions and the crying slowed. Breathing in through her nose and out through her mouth she calmed herself. "Please stop," she repeated.

Whether Mr Derringer had not heard her at first, or dismissed her request, she was not sure. But he heard her the second time and released her hands, looking questioningly at her. Ary drew the walls back up around her and displayed none of her previous emotions to him. It did no good to cry—it changed nothing.

"I release you from your obligation to me."

Another hurt look passed over his handsome face.

"You may consider your duty to me complete. I know who my parents are, and you have helped me to gain a respectable new position through your connections. There is no more I need from you—and I do not wish to stay at Duriel Hall."

Lie. It was a lie. And she felt it deep in her soul. But what she wanted did not matter. Her eyes dropped from his—she could not bear to return his gaze. If she held it too long her resolve might falter.

Her last words appeared to knock him physically as well as emotionally. He rocked back on his feet and rose. Ary could feel his eyes hot upon her. She could still feel the memory of his hands on hers. She clenched her fists to eradicate the feeling. Sentimentality would ruin them both.

"That's truly what you wish?"

"Yes," she lied again. It was a little easier this time.

He waited several long moments, staring down at her, and then he bowed stiffly and said in a curt tone, "Then I will not stand in the way of your wishes. I shall write your reference."

"Thank you," she said, hating the turn in his mood

and wishing they were back to laughing over ancient poets again.

"You know, don't you," he said, in a tone far removed from the emotional one he had used earlier, "that Charlotte and I have set the rumour mill straight? We have fed it with truth, and we can hope that all these tales will die down soon enough. There is no proof of your father's guilt, whatever the Northern Department says. Mr Pinchley said himself there was doubt over the incident. Your father's shame does not have to be yours to carry."

The thought of them defending her made Ary feel the pain of leaving all the more acutely. But she had overheard plenty of chatter last night which did not fall in line with Mr Derringer's version of events. She had still seen whispering behind fans and malicious looks.

"I thank you for the words, but no matter the truth, I carry the shame, for there is nothing to dispute it. That's just this world, isn't it? We carry the sins of our fathers, and we live the lives laid out for us. Mine is not that of a lady."

"You're wrong." Again, his tone surprised her by its forcefulness.

"I don't say it for your sympathy."

He made a groaning noise, and then said, "I know." He sighed. "That is what makes it so much more despicable—that you will soldier on in spite of the injustice."

"We won't see full justice on this side of heaven, Mr Derringer." The words, however true, sounded cold even to her own ears. As if she were preaching him a sermon, not leaving behind a life she had come to love.

"And until then, you still want to leave us?""

"Want is not the right word," Ary replied in a moment of weakness. "I must—to protect you from the damage of knowing me."

He stared at her, saying nothing. Then, without looking her in the eye, he bowed and left the room.

She felt numb. The intense feelings which had ended in her crying just a short time before were locked away now. She stared out the window to where Charlotte was still painting, unaware of the conversation that had just happened in the sitting room. Ary saw her charge in a kind of daze. She tried to resume reading *The Odyssey*, but the words jumbled before her eyes.

When she was gone from here, in her new position in Yorkshire, the control over her feelings would return. The control over her destiny and who could hurt or abandon her would reside once again in her own hands. She knew that was the safest, the most sensible decision, and it would keep those two—whom she had come to care for—safe.

Yet the future she had planned so safely, so carefully, stretched ahead empty and lonely. And the idea that she would not see William Derringer again, that she would not share literary jokes with him, or have him defend her honour—it caused the breath to catch in her throat.

CHAPTER 25

"Inoticed Miss Sade did not speak to m-me this evening," said Charlotte, her words disturbing William's thoughts.

The siblings were cosied up in the rose drawing room, neither ready for bed, both for the same unspoken reason. Ary was leaving tomorrow.

That was where William's mind had been. Upstairs with Miss Giles who had already retired. He wondered how well she would be sleeping tonight knowing that she was leaving them tomorrow. Perhaps forever.

"Oh?" But William was not querying it in truth. He had seen the cut the Sades had given both he and his sister.

The smug look on Roberts' face when he too passed them by, nose held high, not looking in their direction or greeting them even with a nod, had made William's hands itch to strike him.

He couldn't. But the thought of doing so had been strong in that moment. A few more of the Sades' close circle had cut them as well. Though Pinchley hadn't—and for that William was thankful, for he had needed a favour of him.

"Y-yes, I think they did it on p-purpose."

William turned his head to take in his sister's profile, but was surprised to see it not marked with sadness, but more by speculation. She may have been oblivious to the tension at her first assembly several weeks ago, but no longer.

"I think it very silly of them." She was staring up at the ceiling, laid back on the arm of the chair in which she sat, legs dangling over the other, shoeless feet bobbing as she spoke. "To think they will miss finding out what a wonderful woman Ary is all because of their pride and fickle notions of what is important."

William laughed involuntarily.

"Exactly right, sister. If only you had Society's ear, you might speak some sense into them."

She chuckled, putting the glass of sherry to her lips to take a sip, and looking like a decadent queen with her emerald jewels winking at her neck and the voluminous green silk dress billowed around her.

"If I cannot speak sense into Society"—she swung around, her toes grazing the carpet again as she sat upright—"perhaps I might to you."

"Lottie." William said her name with a warning tone.

"She leaves tomorrow for her new position in Yorkshire, and you have said nothing to her, even though I begged her not to take up her new engagement until this month. I would be lying if I said it was only for your sake, for I do not want her to leave either, but I was hoping that in that time you might summon the courage to tell her how you feel. I see how you look at her still. It's much like how Jupiter looks at me when he's longing for me to throw that ball of his."

There was a gleam in her eye. She took another sip of sherry, and then said without the amusement, "You must tell her."

"Lottie, I've told you, she does not want to stay, and I will not manipulate her into doing so only for my own desires. She must have her freedom."

"Duriel Hall is free, and you would not be a tyrannical husband. Besides, how do you know it is just your desire?"

"Lottie, stop it."

"Oh, I know! I am not just trying to provoke you. But you have always tried to do the honourable thing. You have protected me and raised me after Mama and Papa's deaths. I am worried that you have been too seriously focused on those things. Your life cannot just be about mine. You must consider what *you* want."

He wanted Araminta.

"I think," said Charlotte, swinging sideways in the chair again and dangling her legs over the arm in the most unladylike fashion, "you are scared, brother."

William scoffed, rubbing his hand over his mouth and pushing away the sharp sensation his sister had struck in him with that annoying truth.

"I think you are—but think of poor Ary. She will hardly be the one to reach out and say anything when she has no one to catch her if she falls."

Charlotte's words, spoken with such simplicity, were profound. They caused William's mind to go deeper in on itself as he considered them.

"Can we do nothing to persuade her to remain?" asked Charlotte.

Ary had stayed for Charlotte's first assembly as she had promised, and had even delayed going to Yorkshire by several weeks due to Charlotte's pleas, but now she was really going.

Over the past two weeks William had been doing everything he could to make Ary stay. He had not been resigned to her leaving them. He had asked for Mr Pinchley's assistance, but the information he hoped to discover had not yet come to light, and until then, William knew his arguments for Ary to stay were the same as before. He would get nowhere with her.

William had come across Ary in the library several times over the past few weeks. She seemed determined to read every book on the shelves before she left. He had not wanted to intrude on her solitude after she had been so clear in her desire to leave Duriel Hall, so each time he had made an excuse and left.

It had been difficult. But he had no wish to see her cry again, no matter how many fresh arguments surfaced in his mind. None of them included the fact that he loved her. That since she had come to Duriel Hall it had felt as though the home was complete. That he could not imagine being here without her. Doing life without her. That these weeks barely speaking had done nothing to lessen his feelings.

He could not tell her how he felt when he knew that her perception of the harm she was doing to him and Charlotte was making her leave. What good would that do? It would only cause her more distress. Whether she felt for him or not, she would reject him out of hand because of the scandal she believed she was bringing on the Derringer household.

"You do know if you don't tell Ary how you feel then you will be pounced upon by Miss Sade? Once Ary goes —of course—and she is no longer cutting us."

"Charlotte!" William exclaimed in exasperation.

"I am only pointing out the truth," she replied, raising her hands in surrender. "And if you have no intention of speaking to Miss Giles before she leaves tomorrow then you'll have to look elsewhere for a b-bride."

William glared at his sister, but despite her stammer she gave him back stare for stare. Then she abruptly swung back around in the chair to dangle her legs once more.

"My sister," said William, a rueful smile threatening his mouth. "A lady of Society." He swept a hand to take in her dishevelled, lounging state. "And the oracle of love."

"What can I say?" said Charlotte in the voice of a sage. "I have seen two wandering ships and can see their right harbour is this Hall." She stretched her legs out straight, trying to warm her toes with the fire.

"You should at least show her the necklace, William. I thought you meant to give it to her to wear tonight."

"I had thought to." But when he had commissioned the necklace he had thought... it would have looked like an engagement or courtship gift had Araminta worn it tonight.

"I am for bed, but"—Charlotte rose, padding over to William and placing a hand on his shoulder, pressing gently—"please consider what I said."

William nodded. Turning and kissing the back of his sister's hand, he bid her sleep well. She left him there, staring into the fire and contemplating if he really was scared as Charlotte had accused him. Would his fear stop him from telling Araminta how he felt?

CHAPTER 26

The day dawned overcast and cool outside Duriel Hall. Ary was up early, her cases packed, now stretching to a trunk filled with all the gowns the Derringers had bought her. She was clothed in the same worn dress and patched cloak she had arrived in.

She might look the same, but her time at the Hall had changed her. She stood staring up at the stone lettering she had read her first day here,

GOD IS MY HOME

And she pressed the little wooden heart on her wrist with a gloved finger and thumb. To believe in God took faith. To believe God had provided her with a home and a family took faith too. She felt the familiar doubt wash over her. Having such faith was a risky endeavour. It opened her up to be left alone again when things went wrong. She would not be left this time. She would protect those whom she had come to care for deeply.

Looking towards the family sitting room where she had spent time with William and Charlotte, where she had started to become part of their family, her heart grew sadder.

It was over now.

Yes, it was over, and she was angry at herself for allowing her feelings to develop for this place, for these people. For opening herself up to so much hurt when she had known again and again the loss of home and security. But it was done, and she would have to bear the hurt long after she left Duriel Hall behind.

"So you are to leave us th-then?" asked Charlotte.

Ary turned to see her descend into the hall, a wool shawl around her shoulders, and her expression heavy with sadness.

"I am." Ary held out her hands to take Charlotte's and squeeze them.

"I think it too bad of you to leave me before my coming out in London."

Ary smiled, knowing the vexed comment hid a genuine sorrow.

"I had hoped we might persuade you to stay—to make Duriel Hall your h-home."

"I am afraid I do not have a home," Ary replied, her voice soft and a slight mist in her eyes. "But I shall always count you a friend, if you do not object to me doing so."

"Of course not," said Charlotte, squeezing Ary's hands so tight it hurt and then pulling her into a crushing embrace. "You must write to me as soon as you arrive. Lady Amelia says the country is positively wild up there."

"I will," Ary promised.

As she moved apart from Charlotte she heard

footsteps and Mr Derringer appeared from his study. He bowed formally as a footman came in to say the carriage to take Miss Giles to meet the stagecoach was ready outside.

"Thank you. Please take up Miss Giles' luggage," he instructed, and the young man set to work.

"Here." William turned to Ary and handed her a sealed letter. "Your reference.'"

She took it, forcing a smile. "Thank you."

"William has something else for you," Charlotte said, coaxingly.

Ary saw Mr Derringer clench his teeth and then nod. His eyes were guarded this morning, as they had been since she had told him she was leaving.

He turned back to his study and Ary watched after him. She looked at Charlotte and the young girl nodded encouragingly, gesturing for Ary to follow her brother.

When Ary entered the room, she was reminded again of her first day at the Hall. She glanced to the sofa which she had sat on, where her finger had bled from the rose—where Mr Derringer had given her his handkerchief.

"Here," Mr Derringer said quietly.

He stepped aside so she could see the velvet case on the table. Ary looked around her, feeling as though whatever this was must be meant for someone else. She realised Charlotte had not followed them and she was alone in here with Mr Derringer.

"Please." He held out a hand towards the object on his desk.

Ary looked from the case to him, and seeing his eyes were somewhat softer than they had been, she approached it cautiously. Looking down at the rich velvet she removed her gloves. It didn't feel right to touch it with her worn travelling gloves. She reached out, her fingertips grazing the material. It felt like moss, and without much effort, she folded back the flap of material to reveal another. This too she removed, all the while feeling Mr Derringer's eyes burning into her. Then she saw it, red and glowing, reflecting the light of the room from a hundred faces. A heart. A perfect red heart hanging from a ribbon.

"I had it made to honour your mother, and mine," William said, his voice low. "So that you may always wear a symbol of your token—even to balls and assemblies," he added ruefully. She looked up to see a crooked smile on his lips.

"I don't think I shall be attending many of them in Yorkshire," Ary replied, but there was no humorous expression accompanying the wry observation. "It is too much."

"No," Mr Derringer replied, his low voice immediately firm. "I had hoped to name it the Heart of the Hall."

But she was leaving. That is what he did not say.

"Allow me?"

He picked up the necklace. Ary turned her back to him obediently and he hovered the heart over her head. She felt its weight fall against her chest as Mr Derringer rested the ribbon against the back of her neck, and as he did so, his fingers brushed lightly against her skin.

Sparks emanated from everywhere he touched. Her breath caught in her throat. He finished tying it and she turned to face him, the moment of intimacy over.

"It looks very well on you—and is, perhaps, something to remember us by."

"I shall not forget you," said Ary, a sudden fierceness in her voice.

Mr Derringer smiled, but it was a sad smile. He reached out to her, but stopped short. He opened his mouth as if to say something, but whatever it was died on his lips. She willed him to say it—to allay her fears—to tell her that what she had at Duriel Hall was worth the risk of staying. But she knew it wasn't true. As long as her father was viewed as a traitor, her staying at the Hall would hurt the Derringers.

"I must go to the carriage," she said. "Thank you." She reached up and touched the necklace, and then she turned and left the study.

It was Mr Derringer who handed her up into the carriage, but she did not look him in the eye again. The door closed and her life at Duriel Hall was sealed shut. The wheels of the carriage began turning towards her future.

⁂

"SO LIKE HER MOTHER," Mr Pinchley said.

He had arrived after dinner that evening to find William and Charlotte in the drawing room. The atmosphere was despondent and Mr Pinchley's jovial mood quite at odds with it.

"I am sure you will both miss her," he carried on, still referring to Ary. "Ah, thank you, my boy." He took the glass of brandy William had just poured for him.

"Same determined spirit. I remember when her mother went off and married that soldier Giles. The uproar it caused. But she was certain she was in love, and nothing would deter her. She'll need that spirit with the Matthews children. I hear they've been running their nursemaid ragged."

William waited impatiently for Pinchley to get to the point of his visit. He normally didn't feel so uncharitable, but this evening he was in no mood to host.

"And she leaves right when I hear back from my friend who worked in the government too. Mind you, she seemed determined to have a fresh start and one can't blame her for that, so perhaps it's for the best."

William almost missed the beginning statement.

"What?" he asked impolitely.

"My friend Wareham. Wrote me this very morning. Or it could have been yesterday before the assembly, but I wasn't home, you see. I was out seeing the new Lady Fortnum and her blushing groom."

The joke was lost on William. He leant forward in his seat, his heart pounding, his green eyes bright and fixed on Mr Pinchley.

"What did he say?"

"Fortnum? Nothing that made sense. He's a lovesick pup at three-score years."

"Not Fortnum," William was struggling to control his frustration. "Wareham—what news did he have of Giles?"

"Well, the reason it took so long, you see, is because Giles' commanding officer has since died, and his right-hand man is now serving in his place. Seems that the old commander was a bit of an old soak who had a habit of casting blame on good soldiers he disliked. Giles was one of them. The man now serving in the old boy's place—who was the lieutenant at the time—vouched for Giles' innocence.

"Says he remembers the chap going out sober—pardon the detail, Miss Derringer—to round up the rest of his regiment. Got caught in the crossfire, most likely when their captain turned up three sheets to the wind and lost his temper at the men. The lieutenant says he tried to speak up at the time, but was overruled. Something about the old captain being the son of a lord, or some such—had people on his side to cover up the unfortunate episode. Rumour has it, it was he who fired the first shot."

William could hardly believe his ears. After all the gossip and the malicious rumours, Araminta's father was innocent. The disbelief was followed by frustration and then a great sadness as he realised it was all because of one man's poor actions that Araminta had been torn from both her parents to face the trials of a hard life alone.

"You have it in writing?" William was on his feet now, placing his undrunk brandy on the side table.

"Yes, my boy. Brought it with me as I thought you'd like to see it. As I say, just a shame Miss Giles has already gone. But no doubt it is what she wanted and you may send the news on to her there."

"She does not belong there," William said decidedly. "She belongs here at Duriel Hall."

"Hear! Hear!" cried Charlotte, rising up from her dejected pose and clapping her hands.

All doubt and fear had been erased now William knew he could give Araminta what she needed—the knowledge of her father's innocence. If that was the case, then she could stay at the Hall. He'd even publish this Wareham's letter in the Bath Chronicle if it would mean Araminta would stay.

"You mean to fetch her?" Pinchley asked, surprise marking his wrinkled countenance.

"I do. She must know the truth."

Understanding dawned in Mr Pinchley's eyes. "Ah, I understand, my boy. Off with you. If I were twenty years younger you would have me to compete with."

William ignored this. He would tell Ary the truth, but he could not expect anything in return.

"You will forgive us for leaving you?"

"Only if you will forgive me for staying to finish the brandy in your absence—it's top stuff."

William nodded and Charlotte rose.

"Charlotte, you needn't come."

"I will lend my countenance should Miss Giles choose to return, and besides, she is family, William. I wish to bring her back as much as you."

William did not argue with his sister.

"Very well."

They left Mr Pinchley in the drawing room and William ordered the carriage. After that they went to change. William was thankful a stiff breeze had sprung up in the afternoon and resulted in a clear sky this evening. The sun had already set, but the three-quarter moon would give more than enough light to travel by. In a little under three-quarters of an hour they were away, following the post road north to find Miss Giles.

The question that whirled around William's mind was, when they found Miss Giles, would Mr Pinchley's news be enough to persuade her to come back? There was no certainty she would want to after all she had endured. The idea she might refuse was not one William could bear. Their sole focus must be on catching up to her—*that* they could control— and as for Miss Giles' reaction to their news... well, William hated to admit there were no guarantees.

CHAPTER 27

The following morning, Ary sipped her hot chocolate in the taproom of the inn where the stage had stopped overnight. She had not slept well thanks to damp sheets, but she was pleased at least that there had been no fleas.

She clasped the cup tighter, hoping the drink would warm her stiff fingers. The temperature had dropped, and she had no wish to enter the draughty stage already cold.

"Miss Giles," the landlady said, bustling over to her, and popping another fresh round of bread on the table in front of her customer along with a dish of butter. "I was told to tell you the stage is leaving in half an hour. Your things are already aboard."

"Thank you," Ary said, smelling the bread but feeling no desire for it. She hadn't been able to eat since leaving Duriel Hall.

A burly man in a greatcoat and muffler came in—no doubt, the driver of the stage—and he ordered a hearty meal of ham, bread and a tankard of ale. He was just sitting down to his breakfast and partaking in a loud exchange with the landlord on the state of the roads when Ary heard her name again.

"Miss Giles."

She blinked. That voice...

"Oh, Ary! We have found you!" cried Charlotte pushing past her brother and flinging her arms around Ary before she could turn and take them in.

"Miss Derringer?" Ary gasped, her chin tucked over Charlotte's shoulder, the girl not willing to let her go.

Ary caught sight of William then. He wore old top boots she knew he reserved for going about the estate, a plain wool suit and a half-undone cravat forgotten around his neck. She spied the faint shadow of beard on his jaw, and his hair unpowdered and hastily tied back. Then she caught his gaze—and it went straight through to her core. She had not expected to see him again— she didn't think her heart could take it—and as she saw him now, she knew it could not. She felt it cracking.

"Miss Giles." He said her name and Charlotte broke away from her.

All three of them stood silent for a moment, the bustle and noise of the taproom room happening around them.

William stepped forward.

"May I speak with you?"

"There's a private parlour," Charlotte said, having just exchanged a few words with the landlady. She beckoned them both towards a side door. The landlady showed them into a bare looking room with undressed walls of rough lime, and a plainly made set of chairs around a table.

"I will go and tell the ostler to get your baggage down

from the stage. You may always get the next one, but we would not want your luggage to leave without you," said Charlotte, glancing between her brother and Ary before leaving.

Silence fell in the parlour. Ary looked at the chairs, but did not want to sit. She turned to face William. The look in his eyes brought warmth to her cheeks. Gone was the aloofness of the past few weeks.

"Ary," he said, stepping forward.

"Why are you here?" she asked, her voice involuntarily cracking.

He reached out and took her cold hands in his.

"I'm so glad we found you. I have something to tell you."

He looked... happy. No, more than that—she thought he looked giddy. She stared up at him, bewildered.

"I've come to tell you that your father has been exonerated."

She could not speak.

"I asked Mr Pinchley some weeks ago to contact a friend of his who used to work for the Secretary of State for the Northern Department, to try and find out what really happened to your father. I have the letter." He dropped her hands to take it from his jacket pocket. He held it out to her, crumpled, as though it were some rare treasure.

She took it from him and slowly unfolded it, reading the neat lines of writing. They had been wrong—her father was not a traitor. It said it here in black and white. One of his commanding officers had come forward.

Ary looked up as her eyes traced the final words, and her mouth remained slightly parted, no longer from mouthing the words, but now from disbelief. Could it be that her mother and father were both honourable people? That she was not this pariah as she had been made to feel in the last few weeks.

"Araminta," said William, not taking her hands this time, but displaying such an earnest warmth in his eyes that she felt her skin prickling all over. "Do you see? You have nothing to fear anymore. All we need do is to show this letter and all those who have been speaking ill of your parents will be silenced. You don't have to fear hurting us anymore."

Ary sucked in a breath. Had she been forgetting to breathe? How stupid. But this was all too much. She had steeled herself to leave Duriel Hall and all that she had come to care about. She had told herself that she must not allow the feelings for Mr Derringer that had been slowly blooming within her to overtake her wit. She had resolved to face a fate of obscurity alone in the north of England. She had forced away all those feelings and turned the key on them, but he had come for her, and now they ran wild within her.

"Thank you," she said. "Thank you so much for all you have done for me."

A warm smile broke out on his face and the sight of it sent a thrill through her.

"But I did not just come to tell you the news about your father." His smile faded and it was replaced by a look of intense warmth in his green eyes. "I came for my heart."

A new emotion rocked Ary. Shock overwhelmed her. Had he really come all this way for the jewels? Any peace that had been soaking into all the tension and stress of the past few weeks was stalled. She unconsciously raised a hand to feel where the ruby heart lay beneath her cloak.

"You came for the necklace?"

Had he come all this way to tell her such wonderful news and then take back the gift he had given her. What was wrong with this man?

***

"No," William said, his voice deep, his eyes not on the necklace, but running over every part of her face.

His gaze traced the line of her jaw, fell over her cheeks, followed her brows, slipped down her nose, paused on her lips, and then came back up to her deep brown eyes. How dear these features were to him.

"I said I came for my heart." He took a step closer, then another.

He could feel the air crackling between them. He no longer wore a mask of propriety as her employer. There was no longer any need to hide his feelings for her. He looked at her again with the love that had stirred that night when they had been alone in the library. The feelings he had wrestled with coming to understand.

"What do you mean?"

He stepped closer again. Half a step more and their chests would be touching. He reached his hands up and lightly rested them on the tops of her arms before allowing them to slip down to her hands. He felt her shiver beneath his touch as he did so. Picking up her hands, he held them up between them, pushing his fingers up against her own, pressing their palms together.

"I mean that you have my heart in your hands,

Araminta, and I wish more than anything else in the world that you would bring it back to Duriel Hall with you and consent to be my wife."

He watched with delight as the realisation dawned in all its blazing glory in her eyes. She stared at him, her full lips parted, unbidden tears welling in her dark eyes making them look impossibly larger.

"I don't understand," she whispered.

He had to make her understand. The urge he felt to ensure that this woman knew exactly what she meant to him was so strong it welled up inside him and it would not abate until he let it all out.

"From the moment I first spoke to you, Araminta, I have thought of no one else. You have drawn me in with your quiet grace and I have been awed by your enduring strength. Araminta Giles, I have fallen in love with you so completely that you might as well be wearing my heart around your neck rather than that necklace." He smiled ruefully down at her and saw a becoming blush stealing up her cheeks. "And both you and my heart belong at home, in Duriel Hall."

Ary said nothing. He held her hands to his chest, his eyes searching her face, willing for her guard to come down so he might discern her feelings. A slither of doubt pierced his confidence.

"You cannot love me," she said, looking down and away from him.

Suddenly the reason for her hesitation became clear. She somehow thought she was still below him. That it was impossible for him to care for her, the daughter of scandal who had grown up in the Foundling Hospital.

He released one of her hands so that he could take

her chin and coax her to look at him again. Their eyes locked together.

"I can, and I do."

He saw her eyes widen at the fierceness of his tone. Then her brow creased as if she still did not understand him. What could he do to make her see?

"Araminta, when will you realise the woman that you are? Everyone else can see it, but you. How could I not love you after how you have cared for my sister, protected our family, and shown such selfless love?"

He saw it then, a dampening of the doubt in her eyes, and the faintest glimmer of hope.

"I know I am not worthy of your love," he said, "and if you do not return my affections please just say and I will not repeat them. You will still be welcomed back to Duriel Hall. You will be safe there. There will be no expectations of you." He stepped back to give her space.

The glimmer in her eyes grew brighter, and before he could release her hands, he felt the slightest tug from her. Taking his chance, he slowly bent down, brushing his lips lightly against hers. The sensation was intoxicating. She leaned in, and he pressed his lips fully to hers. He released her hands so he could wrap his arms around her and draw her to him, feeling her small figure fit perfectly against him.

Drawing back, he murmured against her lips, "Marry me, Ary."

He kissed her again, and then he felt her lips drawing up into a smile and she leaned back a little, her eyes dancing.

"Yes, Mr Derringer," she answered, in the tone of an obedient servant.

A deep chuckle rumbled up from William's chest

and he pulled her tighter, kissing her again. And this time it was no tentative brush of the lips. He kissed her with all the desire he had felt over the past few weeks but not allowed himself to express, and he finally ran his hands up into that thick dark hair of hers. He heard a pin drop to the floor but neither of them cared. He felt the pleasing sensation of her hands now embracing him, coming up to his shoulders and then his neck, her fingers tickling the beginning of his hair.

"Oh, splendid!"

The couple broke apart at the interruption. William rubbed a hand over his mouth, and glanced at Ary who was busy patting down her slightly wild hair. Both of them were blushing furiously.

Charlotte stood in the doorway, with one of the inn's ostlers standing gawking behind her, Ary's luggage in his arms. A wonderful smile spread over Charlotte's face.

"I have always wanted a sister, and I would certainly have chosen you of all the ladies of my acquaintance, Ary!" Charlotte rushed over to Ary to embrace her.

William saw Ary blush even more thoroughly. It caused his smile to grow even wider.

"Yes, I believe I am to be your sister," Ary said.

"And that means no new companion—oh!" Charlotte clapped her hands together. "Wonderful. Didn't I tell you, William?"

Her brother sighed and rolled his eyes at his sister, though while he was doing so, he was also snaking his hand around Ary's waist and drawing her to him again.

"Yes, Charlotte, yes. Now who's for breakfast? I'm famished and the sooner we can get home the better."

Charlotte went off immediately to find the landlady

again, all stammering and nervousness apparently disappeared.

Ary turned in William's protective arm and looked up at him.

"Home, William" she said with a sigh of contentment, a mist in her eyes and a joy-filled smile spilling out onto her lips.

"Yes," he replied, smiling down at her. "Home"

And then he bent to kiss her once more.

EPILOGUE

"He's moving again, William," Charlotte said, looking up from where she lay sideways on one of the chairs, her stockinged feet hanging over the arm.

William had given up telling Charlotte to sit with more propriety while the painter was here, for she paid him no heed. Ever since her Season in London she had become abominably confident. William was proud.

"Come here, Jupiter." Ary called the errant dog back from where he was wandering off to and patted the blanket-covered dais for him to come and lay down again.

"I wish *I* were able to wander off now," William murmured to Ary.

They were sitting for their wedding portrait and the painter was taking a great deal of time getting their likenesses.

Araminta sat on a winged chair, her husband at her side, his hand resting on her shoulder. Behind them a backdrop of green velvet drapes and an artistically placed faux Corinthian column provided a classical but plain background so as to show the sitters off to their best advantage.

"Soon, my dear," said Ary.

"If you were not so insistent on the dog being in it we would be done by now," he muttered.

"Stillness please!" called the painter, his face peeping around from the canvas to scold them.

"Ordered about in our own house," William said, ignoring the stricture, "and subject to a dog's whims. What has the world come to?"

"You did choose to marry a common soldier's daughter, William. What did you expect?" asked Ary, amusement in her voice.

"I chose to marry the best woman of my acquaintance," William replied. "I will consider all hardships worth that particular triumph."

Now Ary completely ignored the painter, and swivelled in her chair to look up at her husband.

"And I am very happy we are married too," she said, grinning up at him, a wonderful lightness in her countenance that had not been there before.

William caught sight of the heart necklace. They were both wearing red to complement it—Ary in a red silk dress and he in a dark red silk suit. Since giving it to Ary, William had added a jewelled chain to the necklace on their wedding day, to replace the ribbon from which the ruby heart hung. The addition had made it the most expensive family jewels the Derringers now laid claim to. The Derringers. Ary was now Araminta Derringer. He swelled with pride. But as he looked down at her, he knew the necklace was not the most precious family jewel. No. That was Ary.

"You look very beautiful today, wife."

"Please be still!" the painter called again.

"No," William replied, taking Ary by the hand and escorting her from the dais. "That's enough for today. I wish to go and walk in the garden with my lovely wife. Jupiter!" he called, the dog ecstatic to get off the dais and follow them out, his tail wagging.

"I think we made him angry," Ary said, giggling as they left the room, the painter complaining under his breath.

"Don't be too long," Charlotte called after them, "Mr Pinchley will be here soon for dinner."

"Yes, Lottie," Ary and William called in unison.

They strolled through the house, arm in arm, and out into the gardens where the roses were once again in bloom.

Ary bent to smell one on the way past.

"Careful, my love—we know what happened last time."

"Ah, yes." Ary straightened, turning and smiling coyly at her husband. "I still have that handkerchief."

"Do you?" William asked, brows rising.

"Yes, it was the first thing you gave me."

"That's not true," William countered, "The first things I gave you were those three books to read."

"Oh, so it was." Ary tapped a finger to her chin, a teasing light in her eyes. "And then you gave me your heart."

"I did." William spoke with a more earnest tone. "And you gave me yours. But enough of this lovemaking chatter. I got you away from that painter for a very specific reason."

"Yes?" she asked, an enquiring look on her face.

"To kiss you."

And with that, he took her in his arms and bent to the task at hand.

THE END

REVIEW THIS BOOK

Thank you for reading *Finding Miss Giles.*

If you enjoyed it, please share your review on Amazon, BookBub or Goodreads to help other readers find my book.

READING GROUP RESOURCES

Would you like to enjoy this book with your reading group? The *Hearts of the Hall* novellas each come with reading group resources.

Visit **heartsofthehall.com/reading** to download your discussion questions for *Finding Miss Giles* and the other books in the series.

GLOSSARY

Arabian Nights' Entertainment - One Thousand and One Nights is a collection of Middle Eastern folk tales compiled in Arabic during the Islamic Golden Age. The first English language edition (c.1706-1721) was entitled *The Arabian Nights' Entertainment.*

Assembly – the Assembly Rooms in Bath were a social hub for Georgian Society. They offered subscribers two balls a week during the Bath Season, you could pay extra for tea, and there was a card room for gaming. There were several sets of Assembly Rooms in Bath. The rooms appearing in *Finding Miss Giles* are the Upper Assembly Rooms, designed by John Wood and opened in 1771.

Bamming – to hoax, trick, cheat or fool someone. 'To bam someone' or 'bamming someone' was a shortening of the word 'bamboozled' and slang commonly used in the 18th century.

Cerulean – a shade of blue resembling the sky.

Cravat – usually a strip of linen that was tied around a gentleman's neck, the equivalent of a tie for the 18th century gentleman.

Crossbow – a weapon similar to a bow and arrow, often used with a mechanism to draw the bow string back, and which fired bolts. They were popular in the Middle Ages. The crossbow mentioned in Duriel Hall's collection is based on a c.16th century crossbow, which Philippa saw in armoury at Arundel Castle, West Sussex. As the crossbow has an ebony frame with ivory decorations inlaid, it was likely a fashionable hunting weapon, rather than a practical weapon used in battle.

Duriel – a Hebrew name meaning 'God is my home'.

Foundling Hospital – Thomas Coram campaigned for seventeen years to receive a Royal Charter from King George II to create the Foundling Hospital. Established in 1739, the Hospital looked to care for babies at risk of abandonment in London, of which there could be around a thousand a year.

Globes – globes often came in pairs in the 18th century. One globe was 'terrestrial' meaning it depicted the earth and the land, while the second globe would be 'celestial' depicting the stars and constellations.

Grand Tour – a customary trip taken through Europe by young men of rank usually when they came of age at twenty-one years old.

Illuminated manuscript – a book whose pages have been decorated by flourishes and illustrations in rich colours like gold, silver, blue and red. They were predominantly created during the middle ages and while sometimes the images were purely decorative, they could also highlight specific passages and enhance their meaning.

Inigo Jones – was an English architect (1573-1652) who brought the classical architecture of Rome and the Italian Renaissance to Britain. In *Finding Miss Giles*, Ary has read a book by Inigo Jones and John Webb entitled *The Most Notable Antiquity of Great Britain, Vulgarly Called Stone-Heng, on Salisbury Plain, Restored, (London, 1655)*, in which Inigo talks at length on the classical architecture of ancient Rome.

On dit – a piece of gossip.

Ostler – a man employed by an inn to look after the horses.

Portico – a porch leading to the entrance of a building with a colonnade styled on that of ancient Greece.

Portmanteau – a leather travelling bag. The word is a compound of 'porter', meaning to carry, and 'manteau' the French for cloak.

Renaissance triptychs – a triptych is a piece of art made of three panels that can be folded shut. Triptychs were often used as altarpieces in churches, displaying biblical scenes with lesser scenes flanking a central, often larger, scene. The Renaissance period which linked the middle ages to the early modern (approximately between 1400-1700), saw a flourishing of European culture and art.

Robe* à *l'anglaise – a closed-fronted gown. This type of garment fastened in the front over structured undergarments.

Robe à la française – an open-fronted gown. This type of gown did not meet in the front. It would be worn over a matching petticoat and stomacher.

Robe à la turque – inspired by the fascination with 'exotic' Turkish influences, this gown had skirts of a different colour to the petticoat, sleeves and bodice. The skirt tended to be longer, forming a train, and a sash was often tied about the waist. The bodice would have long sleeves and the wearer could pair it with a turban to complete the ensemble.

Season – the Season was a period of the year when the upper classes of English Society would gather and host social events such as balls. The London Season coincided with the sitting of parliament, meaning most aristocrats were in London with their families. The Bath Season generally ran from October to early June.

Secretary of State for the Northern Department – prior to the formation of the Foreign Office in 1782, foreign relations were divided geographically between the Northern and Southern Departments. The Northern Department oversaw foreign relations for the

Netherlands, Scandinavia, Poland, Russia, and the Holy Roman Empire, while domestic affairs were shared with the Southern Department. The Secretary of State for the Northern Department in 1780 was David Murray, The Viscount Stormont.

Soak – as in 'old soak' refers to someone who is a drunkard.

Stomacher – a stomacher was a 'v' shaped piece of material worn at the front of the bodice to fill in the front of a *robe à la française*. It was generally boned or pad-stitched and the gown was either pinned either side or sewn closed when worn.

Stucco – a decorative plaster that was used on walls and ceilings, often with added sculptural and artistic elements.

Token – until the 1760s, mothers leaving their babies at the Foundling Hospital would also leave a small object as a means of identification in the hopes they would one day be able to return and reclaim their child. There are thousands of tokens still in existence in the Foundling Museum's collections and archives, and it is one of these extant tokens which I was inspired by when imagining Ary's heart token.

Philippa Jane Keyworth, also known as P. J. Keyworth, writes historical romance and fantasy novels you'll want to escape into.

She loves strong heroines, challenging heroes and backdrops that read like you're watching a movie. She creates complex, believable characters you want to get to know and worlds that are as dramatic as they are beautiful.

Keyworth's historical romance novels include Regency and Georgian romances that trace the steps of indomitable heroes and heroines through historic British streets. From London's glittering ballrooms to its dark gaming hells, characters experience the hopes and joys of love while avoiding a coil or too! Travel with them through London, Bath, Cornwall and beyond and you'll find yourself falling in love.

Keyworth's fantasy series The She Trilogy unveils a world of nomadic warrior tribes and peaceful forest-dwelling folk. Explore the hills, deserts and cities of Emrilion and the history that is woven through them. With so many different races in the same kingdom it's become a melting pot of drama and intrigue where the ultimate struggle between good and evil will bring it all to the brink of destruction.

More at:

philippajanekeyworth.com

amazon.com/author/philippakeyworth

instagram.com/pjkeyworth

facebook.com/PhilippaJaneKeyworthBooks

twitter.com/PJKeyworth

tiktok.com/@philippajkeyworth

bookbub.com/profile/philippa-jane-keyworth

goodreads.com/philippajanekeyworth

A DANGEROUS DEAL

(LADIES OF WORTH, BOOK 2)

Lady Rachel Denby is in need of a husband and a chance encounter with the reserved Lord Arleigh inspires her to offer him an outlandish deal.

He will save her from impending financial doom and she will help him gain his inheritance. All they have to do is marry. It sounds delightfully pragmatic. Yet as they embark upon their matrimonial bliss, they find that being husband and wife is anything but simple. Pleasing the stiff family relations, keeping a nosy sister in check, and dealing with unhelpful solicitors complicates their deal. To make matters worse, there are unplanned feelings growing between them. But the unorthodox Rachel can't help engaging the aloof Viscount, and his Lordship is certainly not the cold fish he at first appears. Suddenly, the deal they made is far more than just a practical solution to their problems, it's fast becoming downright dangerous!

This is the second book in The Ladies of Worth series of Georgian romances. It centres on the sister of Lady Rebecca Fairing from Fool Me Twice, and you'll get to see Caro and Felton again, and let's not forget the shrewd Lady Etheridge and her wicked wit!

http://mybook.to/ADangerousDeal

LORD OF WORTH

(LADIES OF WORTH, BOOK 3)

London 1776: Lord Worth is busying himself restoring his family fortunes and burying any feelings he still harbours for the woman who rejected his proposal.

The fact that the lady in question
—Lady Rebecca Fairing—
happens to be his sister's best friend, his niece's godmother, and present at every Societal gathering of consequence is... unfortunate.

Meanwhile Rebecca fears she made the wrong decision in rejecting James Worth, but when he assures her he won't be renewing his proposal, she is forced to accept her choice. It doesn't take long for the eligible Lord Worth to attract other suitors, among them Lady Sophia, daughter to Society's most notorious gossip, Lady Goring.

Rebecca knows she must step aside and allow James to find happiness, but when she senses all is not as it seems in the Goring family, she can't help but intervene.

As James and Rebecca work together to unearth Societal secrets, deal with scheming matriarchs, and face villainous highwaymen, they find themselves more in each other's company than ever before.

Will they continue to bury their feelings for one another, or will they finally realise what it means to love?

http://mybook.to/lord-of-worth

Want to read more by Philippa and be the first to hear about book bargains and giveaways?

Sign up to her newsletter at:

philippajanekeyworth.com

ENGAGING MISS SHAW

Book 2 in the Hearts of the Hall series

He's desperate for a governess. She needs to escape her matchmaking sister.

Bath 1815: John Derringer doesn't need a wife, and he certainly doesn't need children. Devoted to studying ancient Rome, all he wants after the death of his brother is to disappear into his research. But now he must take on the family estate—and care for his orphaned nephew.

Unable to see past his grief, John cannot face the boy, leaving him to a succession of governesses who fail to tame the unruly youngster.

Evelina Shaw is resigned to staying unmarried. With no dowry and little beauty, the only men she has attracted are widowers wanting a capable woman to look after their children—and she refuses to settle for that.

When she hears of Mr Derringer's desperate need for a governess, Evelina seizes the opportunity to escape from her sister's futile matchmaking.

But on arriving at Duriel Hall, Evelina can see hurt and misunderstanding everywhere she looks. As she helps bring healing to the Derringer family, her life becomes entwined with theirs, and neither John nor Evelina can predict the consequences...

A story of hope and forgiveness set in the time of Jane Austen.

heartsofthehall.com/engagingmissshaw

RESTORING MISS HASTINGS

Book 3 in the Hearts of the Hall series

Devastated by loss... a stranger takes her in. But will her presence ruin his plans to restore all he's lost?

Harriet Hastings has nowhere left to turn: after losing both her parents within a few months of each other, she is penniless and alone. So when a distant relative makes arrangements for her future, Harriet faces another loss — leaving the place she calls home to go and live with strangers.

Edmund Derringer's on a mission: to restore the family heirlooms he pawned to cover the debts of his failed speculation. The last thing he needs is to be saddled with his cousin's ward — a friendly chatterbox who intrudes on his time, distracting him from the task at hand.

But when outside forces threaten their burgeoning fondness, each will be compelled to re-examine what they really believe about one another, and what their most important goal for the future truly is...

heartsofthehall.com/restoringmisshastings